NEAR LIFE EXPERIENCE

Dave Turner

Aim For The Head Books

Aim For The Head Books
149 Long Meadow
Aylesbury, Buckinghamshire, HP21 7EB

www.daveturner.co.uk

ISBN: 978-1-8383810-0-4

MONDAY

DEATH WOKE AND opened his eyes. Then he shut them again.

Eyes open. Eyes shut. Eyes open. Eyes shut.

That's weird, Death thought. *You usually need eyelids to do that. And while we're on the subject, sleeping's pretty new as well.*

Last night was a blur. Death remembered opening a bottle of whiskey, but had no memory of finishing it, as usual. He put his eyes into the 'on' position and saw only white.

Oh great. I'm blind. Relief came a second later when he realised some kind of fabric was draped over his head and body. A body that felt bulkier than he was used to. He located his hands, which were - as standard - still attached to the end of his arms, and tugged at the tarpaulin until it slid smoothly onto the floor.

He lay on a metal trolley in a cold, white room with small doors built into one wall. Death was familiar with a mortuary. He raised his head and looked down his body and gasped.

This was not *his* body. This one was a lot meatier than he was used to, for a start. His stomach rose and fell beneath the plaid shirt, in time with the air alternately entering and escaping his nose.

Record scratch.

What the hell was he doing with a nose?

He touched his face with unfamiliar pink hands, the muscles and tendons moving unnervingly

3

beneath the skin. Nose, lips, tongue, eyes, ears, it all seemed so flimsy and soft under his fingers.

Death guessed he was alone in the mortuary storage room because there was no screaming or running around at the sight of him moving. They'd assumed this body to be dead, and it would be prudent to get out of here before somebody turned up. This kind of scenario got people asking lots of questions. Questions Death didn't have the answers to.

He raised himself up onto reassuringly bony elbows, swinging his legs over the trolley's side and onto the floor. Transferring his weight onto his feet, he shakily stood up. So this was gravity. He'd read about it and seen its effects in the most gruesome ways, but he never thought he'd ever experience it. He wasn't a fan. Each step he took towards the room's exit was as though walking through syrup.

He opened the door and looked out onto the mortuary's reception area. Nobody was around so, stepping as lightly as he could, Death crossed the floor to the double doors on the other side and slipped out into a long, deserted corridor.

Mortuaries tend to be in the basement of hospitals, so Death's first task was to find some stairs. That happened soon enough, and he climbed upwards, moving directly opposite the earth's pull, which seemed insane to him. Glad to reach the landing on the main level, he peered through the window of the door leading to the stairwell and saw a sign pointing to the exit. This part of the hospital was busier. Visitors, patients and staff all travelled along the corridor - with what Death now regarded as superhuman speed - as he stepped into the traffic.

He staggered clumsily, unable to get the hang of the weight of this new body or how its limbs operated. It was like trying to drive a manual-geared wreck after a lifetime behind the wheel of an automatic supercar. He grew more and more frustrated with each step until he stamped his foot in a fit of temper.

'Can I help?'

Death limped around in a circle until he faced a woman dressed in scrubs. She was pretty, with a slender figure and comforting smile; things that Death wouldn't normally notice in a human, but he guessed he now had to deal with the added fuss of hormones.

'I'm fine, thank you, doctor.'

'It's nurse, or more accurately, Emma.'

'In that case, I'm fine, thank you, Emma.'

'It's just you seem upset.'

'Oh, it's nothing. I was visiting someone. He passed away.' At least, that's what Death guessed had happened before whatever caused his current predicament.

'I'm very sorry to hear that.'

'We hadn't known each other for very long, but it still gets to you, doesn't it?'

'It does.'

Death glanced over the Emma's shoulder, making sure there were no mortuary attendants with big nets making their way towards him. 'Well, I'd better get home.'

'And are you okay to get there?'

He gave her a brave smile. 'I'll be okay. I'll give my friend a call to come and pick me up.'

'That's a good idea.'

When Emma placed her hand on his shoulder, Death wasn't prepared for the small emotional bomb that detonated in the pit of his stomach. It wasn't just physical contact; it was a connection. His frame of reference was obviously tiny, but when their eyes met, he briefly understood the link between all living things.

Death came to his senses. That was enough existential revelations for one day. He needed a cup of tea. 'Thank you, Emma.'

Death turned on his heels and headed towards the exit with what he would almost describe as a spring in his step. That disappeared when he got outside and realised he didn't have a mobile phone on which to call Dave.

'HOW DO YOU lose a whole bloody building, Kelvin?' asked DCI Sam Graves.

'No idea, guv. Carelessness?' Kelvin replied with a shrug.

Sam stared out of the large window at Division Headquarters and sighed. The building had been remodelled into a bright, modern workplace; an open-plan office. Transparency in modern policing. Sam was behind these changes, except when D.S. Kelvin's crisps packets and coffee mugs encroached onto his workstation. He'd set up barricades using ring binders and staplers, but somehow the snack detritus found their way through his defences.

Sam sighed and ran a hand through his thinning hair. With the other, he smoothed down the edges of the moustache he was trying out. He wasn't sure it had been a successful project. In his late thirties now, Sam had been part of the Metropolitan Police Force for seventeen years. His ancestor, Alfred Graves of Scotland Yard, was a hero from the early days and every generation of Graves since had offered one of its own to the thin blue line. Sam's father half-joked that it was the Graves family curse, along with male pattern baldness and supporting Crystal Palace.

After he'd got a half decent history degree from a half decent university, it was Sam's turn to don the uniform and he did so with pride. He'd imagined he'd be a tough cop who didn't play by the rules, but soon realised that not playing by the rules meant a ridiculous amount of paperwork. So he made sure he was methodical, thoughtful and honest. He'd risen through the ranks and was respected by the officers above and below him, who knew he'd get the job done with the minimum amount of fuss. He'd never slid over the bonnet of a car, developed a drinking problem, or become a tortured divorcee. In fact, he'd never married. Not because he was married to the job, or anything like that. It was just hard to meet people in the city.

Instead of becoming disillusioned and desensitised to the work, it was getting weirder. Take the current case he was working on. Just over a week ago, UberSystems Tower in Canary Wharf vanished. It didn't collapse, implode, explode, or one of the other things a building is meant to do at its end. It was there one moment and then gone the next. Structural engineers crawled the site, and they confirmed it seemed as if the skyscraper had been cut out of reality. Forensics had produced no evidence: no explosive residue or fire accelerants. They couldn't find even a single foreign fibre on the site. And Sam knew how much Forensics loved a foreign fibre.

The only occupant of the building at the time was Conrad West, CEO of UberSystems International and - if the popular press was to be believed - renowned bastard. He was a friend and confidante to the great and good, including the prime minister. There was pressure from above to wrap the case up as quickly as possible. One line of enquiry was a connection to the slaughter on the premises earlier in the year but until some fresh evidence came to light, the building and its owner had just disappeared without a trace. Sam was befuddled, which was disconcerting for a man who was usually unfuddled. There was always a trace left behind; a first breadcrumb in a trail that led to the answer. Just ask Louise Corsini, whose kidnap he had solved when he found one of her earrings down the back seat of her ex-boyfriend's car. Sam smiled to himself. That was a good result.

Sweeping prawn cocktail flavoured crumbs into the waste bin, he read the few updates that had trickled into the computer system. They'd logged new CCTV footage from the foyer of an office across the road. Sam made a note to review it when it had been uploaded.

D.I. Moynahan sauntered up to Sam's desk, interrupting his train of thought.

'The commander wants to see you,' he said with a sly grin. 'I wouldn't want to be in your shoes.'

Sam groaned and took his jacket from the back of the chair. Kelvin already had a packet of cheese and onion crisps out from the drawer. 'Don't get any of that near my desk. I've just cleaned it.'

He took the lift to the fabled fifth floor where the senior officers worked. He'd never met Commander Collins, but the feeling amongst the rank and file was that he wasn't a proper copper, just a politician brown-nosing his way to the top. He couldn't detect his own arse with both hands, a map and a torch. Sam smoothed his hair back and knocked on Collins's door.

'Come in!' a voice barked. He opened the door and stepped through into the office.

'You wanted to see me, sir?'

Collins looked up from his work. 'Graves, is it?'

'Yes, sir.' Collins beckoned him in. The office was bigger than his flat and in the time taken to cross the deep carpet, he picked out a few key clues about the personality of the man sat behind the imposing desk. The desk, like the other items of furniture in the room, was traditional: leather and dark wood. No family pictures hung on the walls, only photographs of Collins shaking hands with various dignitaries. Minor awards were lined up on the sideboard at the rear of the room, but the desk itself was clear of any personal items. Collins himself was grey, distinguished and looked good in a uniform.

Collins closed the folder on the desk and moved it to the side. He wanted Sam to know that he was giving the junior officer his full attention. Probably picked it up at a management seminar.

'Thank you for coming, Graves.' Collins didn't offer Sam a seat, forcing him to stand stiffly, hands behind his back, between two chairs. Edwardian, Sam guessed. Mahogany with leather cushions. Nice. 'How's the wife and family?'

'I'm single, sir.'

'Oh. I see.' Collins surreptitiously lifted the corner of the folder's cover to check his notes. 'Just haven't met the right woman yet? Or man. We're very inclusive here.'

'That's very reassuring, sir.'

'It's been an unusual week, hasn't it?'

'That would be an accurate description, sir,' Sam replied, glad to move the subject along.

'Any leads?'

Nothing, Sam thought, but he said, 'Forensics weren't able to find anything conclusive at the scene, sir, but we're following several lines of inquiry.'

Collins sat back in his chair and smiled. 'That's a load of bollocks and we both know it.'

Sam was beginning to like the commander. 'About ninety to ninety-five percent bollocks, sir,' he admitted.

'Do we have anything?'

Sam shrugged. 'A thirty-storey building vanished in front of several thousand witnesses. I'm basically waiting for an evil magician to contact us with his demands.'

'And the press?'

'They're having a field day. The internet is full of conspiracy theories. Mad stuff. Some guy called Nick Broughton is the top trending item. He's been viewed more times than that cat playing the piano.'

'I love that little fella,' Collins replied.

'Yes, sir. He's adorable.'

Collins leaned forward, his elbows on the desk and his fingers steepled in front of him. 'Would you be averse to having an advisor brought onto the case?'

'I'm not sure what you mean, sir?' Sam replied, confused. 'There are still leads I need to pursue.'

Collins waved away Sam's concerns. 'This is not a reflection on your investigative skills, Graves.' He paused, looking for the right words somewhere above Sam's head. 'In the past, when a case that contained - shall we call them - extraordinary elements came our way, there was a group of independent experts that we sometimes reached out to.'

'I don't think we're ready to call the psychics and nutters in just yet, sir.' Collins ignored his subordinate.

'We know them as the Gentlemen of Dubious Activities. I take it you've heard that name?'

Sam nodded. 'Yes, sir, but they're a myth; a story you tell new recruits in the bar.'

'No, they're very real. A division of the Secret Service. Very hush-hush. I worked a case with them in the early eighties when I'd just started out. Odd bunch, but they got results. Three chaps I dealt with personally and some back office bod. With everything that's been going on here for the last week, we need them in as early as we can. The problem is, nobody's contacted them for almost forty years because nobody's had to. I think we can both agree there have been some extraordinary events over the past few months. Perhaps we should knock on their door, don't you think? It wouldn't do any harm.' Collins slid a business card across the desk. Sam picked it up and turned it over. Expensive, weighty and black, embossed with simple white text that said: '1, CROW ROAD'.

'This was their last known address.'

'Sir, I'm more than capable of dealing with this myself,' Sam protested. This must be some kind of wind up: mysterious business cards and shadowy government agencies.

'This is not a decision I've made, Graves. This order comes from the top. Find the Gentlemen of Dubious Activities and enlist their help in finding those passengers. Now get going.'

'YOU'VE HAD A little accident?'

Dave and Melanie had just arrived home from their weekend away when a stranger approached Dave on the street. He appeared to be in his mid-thirties, with matted blonde hair and dressed in a tatty plaid shirt and jeans. Something familiar lurked behind the eyes staring back at him.

'Yes.' The stranger nodded. 'An accident.'

Melanie stopped unpacking the hire car and wandered over.

'Is everything okay?' she asked. Dave sighed in reply. Nothing like jumping straight into the deep end after a weekend away. He looked up and down the rows of Victorian terraces, making sure there was nobody lurking in the bushes. 'How do I know you're Death?' he asked. 'How do I know this isn't some kind of wind-up that will end up on YouTube? Tell me something only you'd know. What's your favourite song?'

'*We Didn't Start the Fire* by Billy Joel.'

'Why?'

'Because it contains the most number of people I've met, edging out *Vogue* by Madonna.'

Dave shrugged. 'Good enough.' He turned to Melanie. 'It looks like Death has got himself trapped in the body of a Generation X-er.'

'What happened?' Melanie asked as Dave poked and pulled at Death's new human face. 'You're a lot blonder than I remember from last week.'

Death blew the hair hanging down over his face. 'Yeah. How you lot get anything done with this getting in the way, I'll never know.'

'Shall we go inside? I think I'll need a lot of caffeine to make it through this conversation,' Dave said as he picked up the bags at his feet. Melanie grabbed his arm.

'What if Gary's in? We can't let them meet,' she hissed.

'Actually, I'm kind of curious to see what happens,' Dave whispered back. Melanie locked the car and the three of them walked up the short path to the front door.

Death stopped in his tracks. 'How rude of me. I didn't ask. How was your weekend? Did you get to relax?'

Dave and Melanie shared a glance. 'Not really,' Dave replied. 'I got a load of running in, though.'

They called Gary's name as they opened the door, but he wasn't in. Dave and Melanie dumped the luggage in a heap in the entrance.

'I suppose I should give you the tour,' Dave said, trying to be a pleasant host.

'It's okay, I've been here before,' Death replied.

'When?' asked Dave, racking his brain for a time when Death had visited his home.

'Don't you remember? It was the morning after your first date with Melanie.' Death slapped his forehead with the palm of his hand. 'No, sorry, my mistake. That was another timeline.'

'There are other timelines?' Melanie asked.

'Ignore me. There isn't a multiverse and there are no other timelines where you and Dave didn't get together.'

'Where we didn't what now?' Dave asked, the colour draining from his face. The air filled with a social awkwardness that only quantum physics could generate.

'Where's that cup of tea?' Death asked, rubbing his hands in anticipation.

Realising he'd run into a conversational cul-de-sac, Dave went into the kitchen. It was in the exact state he'd expected it to be in after leaving Gary alone for seventy-two hours. He ran a suspicious-looking sponge around the inside of three dubious mugs, unsure whether he was just making them dirtier. He opened the cutlery drawer and was sure there were more teaspoons in there than there had been on Friday morning. Probably something to do with this multiverse.

When he'd made the tea to the best of his abilities and the biscuit barrel had been located, Dave carried a tray through to the living room where Death and Melanie sat on the sofa. They stopped talking the moment he walked into the room. Multiverses, he reckoned. He wasn't enjoying these scientific discoveries.

Melanie wiped the coffee table clear of the detritus of Gary's weekend: some slimy, some spiky, some crusty. Dave placed the tray down and handed out mugs. Death peered into the biscuit barrel. He wrinkled his nose, which was an interesting experience for him. He'd never had a nose to wrinkle before now.

'What kind of sociopath puts pink wafers into a biscuit barrel?'

Dave sat down in the armchair opposite. 'So, why don't we start at the beginning?'

Death sat back, munching on a dusty chocolate digestive he'd dug up from the bottom of the barrel. 'Well, I was born of chaos and pandemonium, forged in the fiery crucible of the dawn of the universe.'

'Skip to the end.'

'I came and found you.'

Dave sighed. He was tired and irritable in a way that could only be caused by spending the night as a dog.

'Back up a bit.' He waved a hand at Death's human form. 'How did this happen?'

Death brushed the crumbs from his shirt. 'The last thing I remember with any real clarity was talking to you on Thursday night. Try being human, you said. Evidently I did after I finished that bottle of whisky. So, really, this is all your fault.'

'But whose body is that? Somebody must be missing it. We, as a species, are quite attached to them.'

Death shrugged. 'I'm assuming its former owner doesn't need it anymore and I've borrowed it.'

'So, who are you, then?' Melanie asked.

'No idea.'

'What's it like in there?' Dave asked. 'How's being human working out for you?'

'I'm quite enjoying it. Before, my mind felt like living in a vast mansion where I could do anything, but this is like spending the weekend in a small, snug cottage. It's cosy. No distractions. Also, I keep wanting to scratch this.' Death pointed at his groin. Dave nodded in solidarity.

'Yeah, that'll happen. You're taking this well.'

'To be honest, after millennia of existence, it's interesting to have something genuinely surprising happen.'

'So how do you go back to being, y'know, Death: the whisper on the lips of the damned, the dark companion, ya-di-ya-da?'

'I have no idea.'

Dave sat bolt upright. 'You mean you're stuck like that? But you've got work to do,' he said, panic in his voice.

'I don't know what to tell you,' Death replied with a shrug.

'Have you talked to Anne about this?'

Death stared into his mug of tea. 'I thought this might be more in your wheelhouse.'

Dave sighed. 'Have you annoyed her?'

'No. Yes. I can't remember.'

The front door slammed. Everybody froze.

Gary was home.

'I take it you're back, Dave,' he called out from the hallway. 'Because your shit's dumped everywhere.'

'We're in the lounge,' Dave shouted back. 'It's good to be home in the warm glow of my friend's love.'

Gary entered the room, followed by the odour of whatever meat he was eating from a polystyrene box. 'Move your shit,' he said as a greeting, kicking the chair Dave sat in. He looked at Melanie with a smile. 'How was your trip?'

'Good, thanks. Plenty of fresh air and country walks.'

'It's her shit in the hallway, too. Why are you being nice to her?' Dave asked with a whine.

'Because I like *her*.' Gary stopped, pointed a greasy finger towards Death. 'He's new.'

'Oh, yeah,' Dave replied, flustered. 'This is my boss.'

'Steve,' Death said, standing up and offering a hand which he quickly withdrew when he saw the state of Gary's. He sat back down again.

15

'Nice to meet you,' Gary said.

'How was your weekend?' Dave asked, hoping to divert attention away from Death and any questions that might get asked.

'It was alright. Watched all the Die Hard movies.'

Death scoffed. He couldn't help himself.

'You got a problem with John McClane?' Gary asked, ready to defend the films' honour.

'If Die Hard is the Mona Lisa, the other films are faeces thrown at a wall by a monkey.' Gary processed that for a moment before he broke out into a smile.

'I like you,' he said, offering his enigmatic box of meat. 'Would you like some?' Death shook his head.

'No, thank you. I'm full of biscuit.'

'Do you have anywhere to stay?' Dave asked Death. Then, turning to Gary, said, 'The water pipes broke in the flat above his and flooded the place.'

'I exist in a void empty of stimulus or energy,' Death replied.

'Yeah, I've been to Aylesbury too,' Gary said, licking his fingers. 'Feel free to crash on the sofa for a while.'

'Thank you.'

'Right, I've got things to do. Laters.' Gary spun round and walked out the room, closing the door behind him.

'What are we going to do?' Dave asked. 'There's no Death in the world, which means my workload will increase and I'm exhausted. Not to mention the fact you're walking around in the body of what I can only assume is a dead man.'

'I think you need to talk to Anne,' Melanie said. Death groaned and sank into the sofa.

'Isn't this something you can just do over the phone?'

'No, it's not something I can just do over the phone! She's my line manager,' said Dave. 'She should know about this sort of thing and we can get it sorted quicker face-to-face.'

Death threw his hands up. 'Fine. We'll go. But we're getting an ice cream on the way.'

SWIPE LEFT. SWIPE left. Swipe left.

Anne stared at her phone, making her way through the eligible, and ineligible, bachelors of London with an ever-growing sense of disappointment. Tall men, short men, shy men, confident men, men so horny she'd need to bleach her mobile when she returned home from One Crow Road. Not that there would be many swipes right on the other end. At thirty-six, Anne seemed to exist in some emotional blind spot in the eyes of men her own age. She sighed and placed the phone on the desk, screen face-down. Despite its vast population, London could be a lonely place. Recently, she wondered if she had a thing for the guy who worked in the coffee shop, as she always had butterflies in her stomach when she went in there. But it had turned out she was just lactose intolerant.

Anne stifled a yawn. It had been another late night searching the city for wayward spirits. None had appeared. Even the dead were standing her up. Before going to bed, she tried calling Death one more time. It had been days since Anne had seen him, which would be fine for most people, but concerned her. It infuriated her to know he was wandering around London without a worry, like a teenager on a gap year, while she and Dave tried to stem the tide of undead. She'd done the maths and souls around the world must have been tripping over each other. It had been late Thursday when he'd turned up on her doorstep, drunk and annoying her cat Schrodinger. He slurred his way through describing an argument he'd had with

17

Dave before teleporting into a storage cupboard and getting into a fight with Anne's raincoat. She'd not got Dave's side of the story as he'd been away with Melanie for the weekend. They were an adorable couple and needed a break from this nonsense. Anyway, he was due back in the office tomorrow.

Anne turned her attention back to the open document on her computer screen. She was working on a classification system for the undead ranging from 'Class One: Will Probably Kill You and/or Efficiently Relocate Your Soul to Another Plane of Reality', through 'Class Four: Metaphysically Annoying' and, the lowest, 'Class Seven: Wouldn't Notice if They Passed Through You'. It was a depressing way to spend eternity when Anne thought about it. Unable to concentrate, she closed the document and brought up the news headlines. The website didn't mention UberSystems International or the ex-company's ex-building. The news cycle had moved on, churning through another round of politics, gossip and celebrities. It was fine by Anne if she never thought of that night ever again. She still shuddered at the memory of the inky blackness that flowed through her, enveloping her soul.

She surfed the web (*Do people still say that? What do the kids call it these days? I should ask Dave when he's back,* she thought) until she found herself in the less reliable parts of the internet. One website reported that an unidentified male had died of a cardiac arrest in the Accident and Emergency department of a local hospital and his corpse taken down to the morgue. Several hours later, it woke up, strolled out of the hospital and had not been sighted since.

'Some of them aren't even bothering to wait for us anymore,' Anne muttered to herself. She turned the monitor off and picked up a shoebox sat on the other side of her desk. The words "WARS STUFF.

KEEP OUT." had been scrawled untidily on the lid, but Anne was confident this could be ignored. She'd come across it during a clean up. It was tucked at the back of a cupboard, hidden behind some screenwriting books the Infinite Monkeys had left behind.

Anne was about to lift the lid when she heard the door downstairs open and slam shut. Two sets of footsteps made their way up the stairs. She wasn't expecting anybody, and as she looked for something heavy and blunt to throw the door burst open.

'I just think six flakes is unnecessary,' Dave said to a handsome stranger following him into the office.

'My cone, my rules,' the stranger replied, licking the ice cream around a forest of chocolate in his hand. She recognised the voice immediately and put the stapler down.

'What the bloody hell have you done now?'

Death smiled sheepishly, vanilla ice cream smeared on his lips. 'Anne! How are you?'

Anne folded her arms. 'Better than I'm about to be, I'm guessing.'

'I told you this was a bad idea,' Death whispered. Anne finally noticed Dave.

'Hello. Dave. I didn't expect to see you until tomorrow, but I can see you've got your hands full. How was your weekend?'

'Good, thanks.'

'And the food?'

Dave wasn't sure, but he had a vague memory of chasing a squirrel through the forest the night before. 'It was a running buffet. How's it been here?'

'Quiet. Gave the office a clean. Does someone want to explain what's been going on?'

'Funny story,' said Death. 'I appear to have got myself stuck in this body.'

'Were you drinking when this happened?'

'No, no, no... Yes.'

'You haven't been out in public like that, have you?'

'We got a cab. So how do we fix this?' Dave asked.

'Why are you asking me?' replied Anne.

'That's what happens,' said Death. 'One of us does something stupid and you sort it out.'

'Yeah,' Dave joined in. 'Remember when I accidentally summoned that demon when I made that Thai green curry? You came round and trapped it in the roasting pot? Come to think of it, it's still in there. I should probably check that when I get home.'

Anne let out a long sigh that had been building up. 'I don't know what to tell you boys, but I'm getting a coffee and maybe some cake. It's about time you learned to sort yourselves out. You're both old enough.'

'Yeah, but—"

'Just deal with it. I'll be back later.'

Anne grabbed her coat from the back of the chair and swept out of the office.

A LOT OF things go unnoticed in Death's office. The Grim Reaper shouting at a computer screen because he's unable to download his emails tends to hold the attention. For example, tucked away in the room's corner, hiding behind an old, battered filing cabinet, was a door. Beyond it lay Death's library, full of heavy volumes, unknown to the world's bibliophiles, filled with forgotten knowledge. He'd collected them over the centuries. Some were ancient texts containing magic written by wizards and witches, others were undiscovered manuscripts from history's greatest minds. And there was a copy of *Fifty Shades of Grey* Anne had picked up in a charity shop to see what all the fuss was all about.

Perhaps one of these books would contain the answer to Death's predicament. Somebody must have accidentally fused a demon to a human body at some point. So while Anne was out, Dave and Death sat on the floor of the office, surrounded by stacks of leather-bound tomes, poring over text that hadn't been read for centuries.

'What are you reading?' Death asked over the top of a grimoire. Dave looked at the cover of the yellowing manuscript in his hands.

'I think it's a previously undiscovered Shakespeare play.'

'Really? What's it about?'

'A gang of thieves take over the tallest building in Verona on Christmas Eve and it's up to a local yeoman in the wrong place at the wrong time to stop them.'

'Sounds good.'

'Two thumbs up so far. What have you got?'

'The spell book of Karen of Alcester. I don't understand why every witch has to write a long essay about the versatility of eye of newt before they get to the spell you've opened the book for.'

They continued to read in silence.

'This is nice,' Death said after a while. Dave looked up from an exciting scene where the yeoman was fighting one of the Prussian criminals.

'What is?'

'This,' Death replied. 'We never spend time with each other anymore.'

Dave smiled. It was true they hadn't enjoyed each other's company recently. One reason you agree to work with the Grim Reaper is the opportunity to hang out with him. Life, ironically, kept getting in the way.

'Well, when we get this sorted, we'll make time. We'll get some beers in, watch some movies and chill. Or we can just play catch in the back yard?'

'Thanks, dad. I'd like that.'

They both returned to what they were reading until Dave raised his head again. 'Actually, what are you now? I mean, are you alive or dead? Or undead? Maybe you're a zombie or something. Are bits going to fall off you as time goes on?'

Death considered the question for a moment. 'How would I know?'

'Do you have a pulse or anything?'

'How do I measure that?'

'You've spent thousands of years around dead and dying people and you've never learned to take a pulse?'

'I've never had to. It's a cut and dry operation if I'm involved.' Dave dropped the manuscript to the floor and scooted over.

'Hold your arm out.' Death did as he was told, and Dave held his wrist lightly between his thumb and forefinger. There it was. The rhythm of life faint against his skin.

Dave dropped the arm. 'Yeah, you've got a heartbeat. Does that mean you're mortal now? Does that mean you can die? How do you feel about that?'

'I don't know.'

'You were going to live forever. How are you going to cope with the concept of your own mortality thrust upon you now? It's quite a change in lifestyle.'

Death shrugged. 'How do you all cope with it?'

'We don't give it much thought.'

'That seems to be humanity's answer to a lot of things.'

Dave tapped Death's forehead. 'We need to get you out of there quickly. Where's Anne got to? She's been gone a while. Perhaps we should call her?'

22

Death looked at the clock hanging on the wall. Before today, linear time was just something that happened to other people. He was suddenly aware of existence relentlessly charging forward, dragging him along behind. There was a future now, and he had a past.

'We're not getting anywhere with this,' Dave said, snapping Death back to the present.

'Pardon?'

Dave waved a hand at the piles of books. 'We're not getting anywhere with this.' He sighed. It was only twelve hours earlier that he too had experienced being trapped in another body. He said the only sensible thing he could in this situation. 'Sod it. Let's go to the pub.'

ANNE SAT AT an empty table in the bustling coffee shop around the corner from Crow Road. She placed her hand on her neck, her pulse coming through in heavy throbs. Her breath was slow and steady as she tried to gather her thoughts. She hadn't signed on for this. Sometimes it was like mothering an idiot child.

Throughout history, Death had taken on many forms in many cultures. In the Low Countries he is known as Peter the Death, while the Hindu scriptures talk of King Yama who carries a lasso to lead souls to the afterlife. Yet no theological text or religious tract conveys how dumb or irritating He Who Rides the Pale Horse really could be.

The mountain people of Bavaria told stories of King Ludovic the Punctual. When Death finally visited, Ludovic offered him a glass of Schnapps. Then another. When they'd finished the bottle and Death was drunk, Ludovic bargained for one extra year of life on the toss of a coin. If it came up heads he won, but if it was tails then Death lost. A year later, they shared a drink as friends and played the game again. This continued for another fifty years.

The one time Anne brought this up, Death told her it was just an old wives' tale. He insisted he'd figured it out after only eight or nine years. He just really enjoyed the Schnapps.

Anne stirred her coffee, letting her anger melt away with the white clouds floating on the surface. They would stew in the office for a while, then she'd go back and sort them out. There must be something they could do. While most people prayed for a world without Death, nobody thought about the admin.

ANNE RETURNED TO an empty office. Someone had stuck a sign reading GONE DRINKIN' on Death's door. Anne cursed as she pushed the door open against the pile of books that had fallen against it. Once she'd made it in, she looked at the state of the room, items strewn everywhere. There was the 'World's Best Death' mug Anne had given him as a Day of the Dead present sat on the desk and a medieval garment with 'My Dad Went on the Crusades and All I Got Was This Lousy Tunic' sewn into it draped over the back of a chair. A piece of the True Cross that Death had been meaning to put on eBay was being used as a paperweight.

When she looked at the spines of the books, Anne figured out what the boys had been up to before they'd got bored and sloped off to the pub.

Life should have got easier once they'd defeated Conquest, shouldn't it? A new chapter in their lives. But that's not how it worked. No drawing a line under things. Life was just one problem bleeding into the next. It was time to deal with the latest one.

With a sigh, Anne sat cross-legged on the floor and grabbed the book nearest to her. If you needed something doing around here, you had to do it yourself.

DR RAYMOND CARROLL stepped awkwardly from the train carriage onto the platform at Canary Wharf. With a small, well-trimmed goatee beard, round tortoiseshell glasses and a black turtleneck jumper, he had a heavily animal-based aesthetic. Hovering by a bench, idly thumbing through a free newspaper, he waited for the other passengers to travel up to the surface. When they'd disappeared, he casually walked the length of the platform. With its chrome and glass, and a latticework of exposed piping hugging the ceiling, he'd always thought the station looked more like a Bond villain's underground lair than a stop on the Jubilee line.

When he reached a door in the wall at the far end of the platform, he took his glasses off and wiped them with a cloth; a pantomime of nonchalance. He cast his gaze around the station one last time. When he was sure he wasn't being watched, he swiped a security card above the keypad next to the door. The lock opened with a clink and, with one swift movement, Dr Carroll opened it and stepped through to the other side.

He waited for a moment for his eyes to adjust to the darkness and then headed down a long corridor dimly lit by lamps embedded in the roughly-hewn rock walls. After a while, he reached another door. He placed his hand on a fingerprint reader and the lock sprang open with a heavy *chonk*. Behind this door was a flight of stairs spiralling downwards. His feet clattered on the open metalwork of the steps as he nodded to the armed soldier stationed at the foot of the stairs.

Several banks of computers dominated the space, their monitors glowing in the half-light. This was the heart of Project Sisko. Buzzing with activity, it was a control room built on a huge budget and a tight timescale. The desks faced a large window opening onto another room carved out of the rock beneath the city. In there, three engineers in white lab coats were tinkering with some kind of machine that resembled an internal combustion engine wrapped in electrical wiring: The Interdimensional Generator Using Multiverse-Mapping Integration, or Thingummy for short. The engineers attached two thick cables to the device. They snaked along the floor, connected to two electrical generators sat on either side, and a steady hum filled the room when they were twisted and locked into place.

Carroll turned his attention back to the computer room. A sign reading 'You Don't Have To Be a Mad Scientist To Work Here But It Helps' had been attached to the side of one desk.

'Excuse me,' Carroll said to the room. All eyes swivelled in his direction. He removed the sign and waved it in the air. 'I know everyone's excited, but can we keep our desks clear of stuff like this? Need I remind you that the minister is visiting tomorrow and we need to show her we're a professional outfit?'

Carroll couldn't blame his staff, all from the R&D wing of the Ministry of Defence. They had constructed all this in under a week, and a giddy exuberance still filled the air as they finally had the chance to move from the theoretical to the practical.

It had been just over a decade since Dr Raymond Carroll had been toiling in the basement of Oxford University's physics department. While undeniably gifted, some in the faculty would say he'd squandered his career obsessing over the science surrounding interdimensionality. That was until the MoD came knocking on his door with a blank cheque, state-of-the-art facilities and all the PhD students he could eat.

Now was the time to show the results of that work. UberSystems Tower, which until recently had stood a few hundred yards from the control room, had been the epicentre of an interdimensional cross rip of immense proportions. The walls between worlds were paper-thin now. The Thingummy sat in the other room, designed by Carroll, was the key to unlocking the whole multiverse and the infinite possibilities that it promised. It would punch holes through realities.

'What's the arc ratio?' Carroll asked a technician at the console next to him.

'We've got it down to between seven and nine, which is within acceptable parameters,' he replied.

'Excellent.' Carroll smiled for the first time in days. 'We're ready to start system testing?'

'Already underway, sir. Cycles one through three have already passed. Once the Quantum Field team is finished, we can move to real-world scenarios.'

Carroll took a chair next to the technician. 'So this is it? We're ready to create a wormhole to another world?'

'I think you know more than anyone that probably won't happen on the first trial, Dr Carroll,' the technician replied. 'This will just be a calibration test.'

Carroll nodded. 'Of course, of course.'

An engineer placed a bowl of petunias on a stool in front of the device and gave a thumbs-up to the control room. They all filed out through a heavy steel door, which they locked behind them with a heavy spin-wheel.

'Area is clear,' announced the tannoy. 'Please take positions.' Everyone standing found the nearest chair to sit on. The technicians typed away on their keyboards, setting parameters and logging commands. An expectant hush settled on the room.

'Real-world scenario One-A starting in five… four… three… two… one.'

There was a noise as if one person in each of the never-ending number of dimensions coughed politely and, in a fraction of a second, the bowl of petunias folded in on itself an infinite number of times and vanished. After a moment of reflection, digits scrolled up the monitor screens. Data gushed into the servers, the network nearly clogging up with ones and zeros. The room erupted into applause, fist bumps and handshakes. Carroll allowed himself a small, secret smile. The tannoy crackled into life again.

'Test successful.'

'ALL I'M SAYING, Dave, is that they should have populated the theme park with only herbivorous dinosaurs. It would have been a lot safer and they still would have made a fortune.'

Dave nodded and said, 'My mother always told me hindsight's twenty-twenty when it comes to Man interfering with what he was not meant to.'

Death looked at Dave over the collection of empty pint glasses. 'Say that a lot, did she? I don't know why there aren't any unicorns in those films, either. They're extinct too.'

'Unicorns were real?'

Death nodded. 'Died out centuries ago. There were also cows that had a single horn.'

'What were they called?'

'Moonicorns.'

Dave was no longer certain how long they'd been drinking. When they'd left Crow Road, they'd walked until they found the first business that would sell them alcohol. It made the cantina bar in

Star Wars look like high tea at the Ritz. Drinkers hid from their problems in the shadows. Looking at someone's pint the wrong way might end up with a beating. It reminded Dave of the first pub they'd hung out in on that Halloween night.

'How did you stop being a werewolf?' Death asked, returning to the subject of their conversation before they'd been sidetracked.

'Melanie broke a centuries' old curse, releasing a coven of witches from magical imprisonment, who then fed me a mystical potion that cured me.'

'That girlfriend of yours is a keeper.'

'She is.'

'No signs of any lycanthropy left, then?'

Dave shook his head. 'Nope. I used to be a werewolf, but I'm all right nooooooow,' he howled. Death choked on his beer, spraying a mouthful over the sticky table.

'I used to know some werewolves back in the fifteenth century,' Death said, mopping his chin. 'Nice guys, but they kept ruining the furniture. Any reply from Anne?'

Dave checked his phone. 'No.'

'So, any words of wisdom for someone who might've become human recently?'

Dave supped his beer as he considered the question. Then he leaned across the table conspiratorially. 'I'll tell you what my father told me. Never eat anything bigger than your own head.'

'That's it? Thousands of years of human endeavours and that's all you can come up with?'

Dave shrugged. 'It's got me this far in life.'

'Yeah, but you spent last night urinating up against trees.'

'It was my weekend off!'

Death shifted uncomfortably in his seat. 'That reminds me, there's a definite pressure south of the border.'

Dave nodded to a door over Death's shoulder. 'There's a toilet over there. Hang on. You've never done this before, have you?'

'I'm sure I'll be able to figure it out.'

'Dude, it'll blow your mind.'

'Any advice?' Death asked as he stood up.

'Keep a barrier of at least one urinal between you and any other people in there and more than three shakes and it's a wank.' Dave giggled to himself.

'Grow up.' Death wobbled over to the toilet door, which he then walked straight into. Corporeality was something he was just going to have to get used to. Rubbing his head, he grappled with the door knob until it sprang open.

Dave sat back in his creaking chair and played absent-mindedly with a beer mat. He tried to cut through the beer fuzz and deal with the matter in hand. As nice as it was drinking with Death, alcohol wasn't a solution to their problems this time. Who could help them with it? It was a little more complicated than asking a mate to help jumpstart a car.

Just then, Death fell back through the toilet door and bounced from table to table like a drunken pinball. It was clear he was struggling with alcohol's interaction with his newly-gained biological and mechanical functions. Before Dave could yell out a warning, he blundered into a gigantic man leaning on the bar, spilling his pint. The bar went quiet.

'Oopsh. Clumsy,' Death slurred, patting the man on the shoulder. Dave buried his head in his hands. They needed to get out of here. Most pub fights are two men pushing the other one away, telling each other to leave it until their girlfriends intervene to tell them it's not worth it. That wouldn't be the case here, though. The man stood up, stretching himself to his full height. It took a while. There was a lot of height to get through. His left hand was missing its little finger, probably the result of some gangland feud, so the tattoos spelled out on the remaining knuckles read 'HAT': an injury that had earned him the nickname Four Finger Freddie.

'Whathefackareyouplayinat?' Freddie barked into Death's face. Dave was up and out of his seat, adrenaline overriding the alcohol in his bloodstream.

'He's sorry about that. We'll get you a drink.' Dave fumbled for his wallet. Freddie realised he would get more sense out of Dave.

'All right. You're lucky. You've caught me in a good mood. Tell your boyfriend to be more careful next time.'

Death peered into Freddie's face. 'I've not seen a forehead like that since the Neanderthals. It's good some DNA made it through. They were nice guys. What they couldn't do with a mammoth wasn't worth knowing.'

'Are you taking the piss?'

'No, I've just done that. You saw me come out the toilet, didn't you? You really have to keep up.'

The fist came from nowhere. Death's head snapped back. When it returned, a trickle of thick blood ran from his nose and dripped onto his shirt. He wiped the top of his lip with a finger and tasted it, making a face at its iron tang. After all the millennia he'd existed, here was another genuinely new experience. Blooms of pain exploded behind his eyes as stinging tears rolled down his cheeks. He could see why humans complained about it so much. It was fascinating.

'Do it again,' he ordered Freddie.

'What?' Freddie replied, confused. People didn't normally bark commands after he'd hit them. They usually did the polite thing of falling unconscious or crawling away, crying.

'I said, do it again.' Death felt his nose. Bolts of agony travelled along nerves until they reached the cerebral cortex, where they made a little home for themselves.

Freddie stared into Death's eyes and didn't like what looked back. 'Who are you?'

Before Death could come up with a cool line, Dave grabbed him by the shirt collar and dragged him out into the cool night.

AFTER HIS MEETING with Commander Collins, Sam returned to his desk, put the business card to one side, swept the crisps away with an antibacterial wipe and carried on working where he'd left off. He couldn't feel anything but insulted. He was one of the best performing officers in the borough, and his record spoke for itself. A high-profile businessman and his skyscraper missing? That's the kind of thing he signed up for. He would crack the case wide open without the help of any gentlemen, dubious or otherwise, and laugh in Collins's face. Well, maybe not laugh in his face. A self-satisfied grin when he had his back turned, perhaps.

But he had to admit he'd reached a dead end. He'd gone through all the information and he was no further along than he had been a few hours before. Perhaps he just needed a break. In the bottom desk drawer was an old leather journal, the cover cracked and worn with age. Graves of Scotland Yard's diary. A burgeoning interest in the history of the Met had inspired Sam to take his great-great-grandfather's paperwork from out of the loft, and he was now scanning the entries so he could digitally store them. When the leather and paper rotted away, the thoughts would survive forever. Sam opened it where he'd left off, the satisfying crinkle of the book's spine sending a small shiver up Sam's own, and read:

'22 December 1874.

Still no developments in the curious case of the missing Fairchild boy. Summoned to Downing Street where I had the honour of meeting the prime minister, a friend of the victim's mother. He has generously placed some resources at my disposal.

Individually, they go by the name of Messrs Conway and Hungerford. Along with Mr Warfield and a mysterious fourth person, they collectively go by the name of the Gentlemen of Dubious Activities.'

The diary fell from Sam's hands. His head swam as the blood in his body decided it all needed to be nearer his feet and would not wait for his brain to keep up. When the world stopped bobbing and floating, he picked up the diary and re-read the passage. He hadn't imagined it. There the name was in his predecessor's spidery handwriting. Sam frantically searched the desk until he found the business card under a packet of cheese and onion crisps. One Crow Road. It looked like he'd be paying a visit tomorrow morning after all.

DAVE AND DEATH sat on the kerb eating takeaway food. Twists of tissue paper were pushed up each of Death's nostrils and the chilli sauce stung his split lip. Passers-by looked at them with expressions ranging from disgust to barely-concealed glee. Death didn't mind. For obvious reasons he was never the centre of attention, even within the Four Horsemen of the Apocalypse, and it amused him that so many pairs of eyes were fixed in his direction now. Maybe that was the booze talking. This human body didn't process alcohol well. It would probably also explain why he thought this kebab was the greatest food he'd ever eaten.

'Good kebab?' asked Dave.

'S'alright.' Death shrugged. 'How's your burger?'

'Overdone.' One side effect of spending a night as a werewolf was a constant craving for red meat; the bloodier the better. He'd asked the guy behind the counter merely to wave the beef burger in the general direction of the grill before serving, but he'd over-cooked by a few seconds.

'What do we do next?'

'Traditionally, we fall asleep on a night bus and wake up at the depot.'

'Sounds like a plan.'

Dave's phone rang. 'It's Anne,' he said, looking at the screen. 'I'll put it on speakerphone.' Dave braced himself and answered the call. 'Hello!' he said as soberly as possible.

'By my calculations you should be wandering the streets eating kebabs around about now,' Anne replied.

'Ha! No! You're wrong!'

'Yeah,' said Death. 'We're sat down.'

Dave slapped Death on the arm. 'What's up?' he said into the speaker.

'While you've been on the lash, some of us have been working. I've found out what we need to do. You should come over. It's best said face-to-face.'

'But you're over the other side of town,' Dave whined. 'Can't you just tell us now?'

'Okay,' said Anne. 'You'll have to kill Death.'

'We'll be right over,' said Death, ending the call.

ANNE OPENED THE door.

'You've been human for less than twenty-four hours and you've already got into a fight?' she asked, looking Death up and down.

'What can I say? I'm a people person.' He collapsed on the couch. Schrodinger the cat, who'd been curled up in a fort of cushions at the far end, woke with a start. He yawned, stretched and looked at Death. A cat knows an abomination of nature when he sees one. Schrodinger raised his hackles, bared his teeth and hissed. When this got no reaction, he tried to maintain his dignity by doing whatever the cat version of a shrug was, and wandered off towards his food bowl.

This was the first time Dave had been in Anne's home. It was exactly as he'd expected it to be. Tidy, with a sheen of the New Age. A handful of old books he recognised from the office were piled up on the coffee table between a large crystal and a TV guide. Anne could tell he was checking the room out.

'Oh, right. You've not been here before, have you?'

'No. It's very nice, but what's that weird smell?'

'Fresh air,' Anne explained, knowing Dave had spent most of his adult life living in an all-male household.

'Hey! Melanie brought a plug-in air freshener with her. Now the flat always smells of Christmas.'

Death gingerly touched his swollen nose. 'Do you have any ice cubes or frozen peas? Something to reduce the swelling?'

'I'll have a look.' Anne headed to the kitchen.

'Feel free to put the kettle on while you're in there,' Death called after her.

'IS THIS ALL you have?' asked Death, pressing a frozen potato waffle against the bridge of his nose.

'Yes,' Anne replied, handing out mugs of tea.

'Fine.' Death turned his head at an awkward angle so he didn't dunk the waffle in the tea. 'So what's this nonsense I've heard about you killing me?'

Anne settled on the floor, her legs folded under her skirt. 'While you two were in the pub, I carried on where you left off. Did you know there's an unpublished Shakespeare play in there?'

'No spoilers,' Dave said. 'I'm only halfway through it.'

'Anyway, I spent the afternoon going through the books and this was the closest thing I could find to your situation.'

Anne picked up the book at the top of the pile and turned to a page marked with an old train ticket. She ran a finger down the thin paper until she came to the paragraph she was looking for.

'Here. In the eighteenth century, there was a case of possession involving a man named Howard Ross. During the exorcism, Howard unfortunately died. A few hours later his body reanimated, telling them he was Asakku, a demon so hideous legend says his presence alone would make fish boil alive in the rivers.'

'I can guess what happened next,' Death mumbled.

'Howard's father removed his late son's head with a sword. Witnesses say the demon left through the neck wound and legged it out of an upstairs window.'

'You want to chop off my head with a sword?'

'That's not fair,' said Dave. 'How come she gets to do it?'

'Nobody is chopping anybody's head off,' Anne replied.

Death nodded. 'Good.'

'Yet.'

'What do you mean, 'yet'? Your plan is to chop my head off, hoping I spring out like some ugly demon from a bloke's head? And this is all based on some three-hundred-year-old gossip? What if it doesn't work and I actually, properly die? Or something worse?'

'I'm not saying we will definitely do it, but it's something to consider.' Anne looked to Dave for support, but he was looking at his phone. 'What are you doing?'

'I'm looking up swords online. Oh wow, you can get one like they used in Highlander.'

'Stop that now,' Anne said wearily. 'Death, tell him to—'

New to the world of drinking in a human body, Death had made the schoolboy error of closing his eyes for over five seconds. He'd slipped into the deep sleep of the drunk.

'Yeah, we should probably get going now,' Dave said, checking his watch. 'Come on, Death. We need to get home.' He shook Death by the shoulder, but that only made him mutter something indecipherable and turn over. Anne sighed.

'You won't wake him up now. Just leave him.'

'Are you sure?'

'Yes.'

'Fine.'

'I'll see you tomorrow.'

'Yeah, see you then.'

Dave let himself out of the flat. Anne slipped Death's shoes off and lifted his legs up onto the sofa, draping him with a blanket she'd found in the bedroom wardrobe. She stood over him for a while. He started snoring. Was this really the creature feared by all mankind?

Leaving a box of paracetamol and a glass of water on the coffee table, Anne went to her bedroom. She lay in bed, staring at the ceiling. She couldn't remember the last time a man, drunk or otherwise, had slept under the same roof as her. And he was very handsome. But no, she thought. He was like an annoying brother. She turned over. Schrodinger nudged the door open and slinked in. He joined Anne on the bed and, curled up with each other, they drifted off to sleep.

TUESDAY

WHEN DEATH SLEEPS, Life wakes from its slumber.

Lightning lit up the sky as it had done the night the first self-replicating organic molecules were fused together. The air swelled as something pushed its way into the universe; a dark shadow with no host. The shape condensed and became more defined. As if an invisible hand sculpted its features, it took a human form.

She existed nowhere and everywhere, in the now and the forever. Beautiful in the way a freshly-forged blade was beautiful, her golden hair shimmered with the light of a thousand dying suns, and the dark suit she wore absorbed the sodium glare of the streetlights.

All around her she could feel life slipping away, the dim light of so many candles snuffed out. Each one a father, a mother, a child, a friend, a lover. All needed the comfort and the closure she provided.

There was much work to be done.

IT APPEARED SOMEBODY was trying to gain access to Death's skull with a blunt, rusty drill bit.

He opened his eyes and the morning sun singed his optic nerves like the Torch of the Damned. He'd had hangovers before, but the difference between a hangover as an immortal being and as a human was like between breaking a nail and losing the entire finger in a woodchipper. His skin was clammy and his throat dry. A blanket had wrapped itself around his legs and his clothes had adhered themselves to his sticky body.

Pulling himself upright on the couch, he waited a second for his brain to catch up. When it thudded back into place, he reviewed the situation. He was hungry. Specifically, he was craving a crisp sandwich. That's what life seemed to be; you're either craving something, waiting for something, or being disappointed by something. He realised he was in Anne's flat because he recognised the cat staring at him.

'Good morning, Schrodinger.' His voice barely registered as a croak. He chugged back the glass of water on the coffee table to lubricate the vocal cords.

'Good morning,' came a reply.

It took a few seconds for Death to realise it wasn't the cat replying, but Anne standing in the doorway to the kitchen. She walked over carrying two cups of coffee and placed one in front of Death. 'How's your head this morning?'

'I can hear a leaky tap two floors up and every drop is like God's bass drum.'

'What do you remember about last night?'

Death sipped his coffee. 'I have a vague recollection of you wanting to cut my head off, but that seems standard these days.'

Anne stared at the carpet. 'It does, doesn't it?'

A cold, heavy stone sat in the pit of Death's belly. This must be one of those emotions humans always bang on about. Chemicals and hormones swirling in a cauldron of neurons and synapses.

'I'm sorry,' he blurted out. It felt almost automatic. Anne patted his hand.

'I know.' They let the moment dwell. A chip slid off the rock in Death's stomach. He was starting to understand how this all worked. Then Anne said, 'Pop your clothes off.'

'What?' Death asked. Was this some kind of ritual of atonement that humans had kept hidden from him?

'Both you and they need a wash. You can have a shower while I put them in the machine.'

'Oh, right, I understand.' Death stood up and started unbuttoning his jeans.

'Not in front of me!'

Death sometimes forgot how self-conscious humans were about their bodies. He understood why. The whole thing was a bodge job, so many parts loose and jiggly, with little thought to the design. Like the appendix, whose only function is to explode and kill its owner. Or nipples. What was the point of them? You could press them as much as you'd like and nothing fun happened, such as the top of your head opening like a pedal-bin.

'Go into the bathroom,' said Anne. 'There's a towel and dressing gown in there. I take it you know how to work a shower?'

'Yeah, I've seen Psycho enough times.'

AS ANNE PUT Death's clothes on a mixed-load cycle, he stepped into the shower to wash away the sweat and beer. As the warm water splashed over the unfamiliar body, he quickly understood why humanity spent so much time under these things. The only disappointment was the shower gel. The label said it contained real fruit extract, but it tasted horrible.

He stayed in there until he used the hot water up. Turning the taps off, he stepped out from the bath and dabbed himself gingerly with the towel. When he'd patted himself dry, he wrapped the towel around his waist. Wiping the condensation from the mirror, Death stared at the blurred face reflected back at him. It was symmetrical, which he believed was an attractive quality amongst humans, but tarnished by the swollen red nose and purple bruising shadowing his left eye. His was a handsome face, but lived in. At least he had his own hair. The stubble prickling his jaw scratched the palm of his hand when he stroked it.

Anne knocked on the door.

'Can I come in?' she asked. Death checked the towel was secure.

'Yes,' he called back. Anne poked her head around. She let her gaze wander over him. This body was a definite improvement on his usual appearance.

'How's it going?'

'Good, thank you. Though I need to get rid of this.' Death pointed to his face.

'Your chin?'

'No, the hair on it.'

'We can fix that'. Anne slipped into the room and opened the cabinet above the sink. She pulled out a can of shaving cream and a razor and put them in Death's hands.

'But that's a woman's razor,' Death protested.

'So? They all work in exactly the same way.'

'But… it's pink.'

'You've already succumbed to toxic masculinity?'

Death sighed. 'Fine. I'll use it.'

DAVE HAD READ that a fried breakfast was an excellent cure for a hangover. And it worked. He felt much better after he'd thrown it up.

He'd woken up on the floor next to the bed, one shoe on his foot and the other found later in the fridge. He showered and changed into clean clothes. Though his body seemed to defy the laws of physics by being both hot and cold simultaneously, Dave stumbled out of the house and down the road in the tube station's direction. The thought of the heat of the train carriage almost made him turn back round, so he picked up a bottle of water from the newsagent on the way and chugged it down as he descended towards the platform at Wren Park station. The ceramic tiles lining the station wall that curved over his head were refreshingly cool when he pressed his cheek against them, unbothered about how it looked to the other commuters.

The train arrived and Dave squeezed himself between the bodies, joining in the daily game of Train Tetris. The doors slid shut, and the train juddered forward into the pitch-black tunnel. It rattled along, the air screaming in the darkness. The lights flickered and fizzed and fear lurked in the gaps in-between. The passengers rocked from side-to-side as the wheels skipped along the tracks. The scream and song of metal against metal raised in pitch and volume as the train picked up speed. Something was wrong. Reality was lurching to the left. Dave had that tingling sensation he got when things were about to get weird.

'The next station is Bethnal Green,' announced the driver as the blackness fell away from the windows. But the signs on the wall read Wren Park. The advertising posters had the familiar crude jokes drawn in marker pen on them. The train had somehow performed a u-turn in the tunnel. And if you usually tried that in a tube train, it made a big old mess.

The doors hissed open, but nobody got on or off. The other passengers wiggled themselves loose from each other and peered out into their shared déjà vu. Then something unusual happened. Murmuring voices filled the carriage, strangers expressing surprise to each other and making eye contact.

'Err… Apologies. This stop is Wren Park. Again...' the voice crackled on the speakers. After a few seconds, the doors bleeped and shut. The train pulled away. 'The next stop is Bethnal Green. Honest.'

THE GHOST OF Mike Dinsdale tried to mutter under his breath until he remembered there was nothing to mutter under. Until recently he was the actual Mike Dinsdale, successful owner of a chain of cut-price fashion outlets and scourge of the unions. And then he wasn't. His last act had been to approve the buy-out of a competitor when he noticed a tightness in his chest and a sharp pain down his left arm. Darkness quickly followed. At least that didn't hurt.

He was no longer the head of his own empire. The realisation stung. Sure, he'd miss Janice, and he'd grown attached to the kids over the years, but his malfunctioning heart belonged to the business.

There he stood next to his own body. He'd stared at his corpse for hours, realising with a sting of regret how much he'd let himself go. No wonder his heart gave up, having had to power all that weight. Nobody called for him, worried about where he might be. Not Janice, nor the kids. They probably assumed he was boozing with friends or staying the night with his PA Tiffany in the flat he didn't know they knew about.

The cleaners found him in the early morning. The police and ambulance crew eventually showed up and proved themselves to be the incompetent shower of bastards he'd always suspected. He shook his head. This was his tax money. Well, not *his* money, obviously. That was sunning itself in the Cayman Islands. Though his personal financial interests annually brought in ten figures, with some accounting sleight-of-hand, he'd been paying less to the Revenue than the cleaner who'd found him.

When the initial investigation concluded there were no suspicious circumstances surrounding the death (and if there were, the list of suspects would be a long one), the funeral home employees unceremoniously placed his body into a plastic bag and wheeled it out on a gurney. One-by-one, the police officers and medical teams left his office until Mike was alone.

Before his body was cold, the financial director Vince McKay had been measuring the office for curtains. It made sense that he should take Mike's place, but have a little respect, yeah? The boss just died. Still, he could spend the time haunting him and slowly driving him mad. Mike spent the best part of the week trying to carve terrifying messages into the wall, but the decorators just painted over them.

He always thought that, when he died, he'd wake up in heaven (a slim possibility), or hell (more likely), or reincarnated (not French, please). He'd been raised C of E, but had never really committed himself to that or any other religion. You don't sign the first contract that comes your way, do you? You search the market for the best deal. He just hadn't got around to it yet. He'd assumed he'd have more time. He didn't expect to be abandoned for eternity.

'Hello?' he called out into the ether. 'I'd like to register a complaint.'

Nothing. He didn't know how the hierarchy of the afterlife worked, but as soon as he found someone in management they'd be getting a piece of his mind. This wasn't how you ran an organisation.

Maybe it was because he was new money. It had taken him years to get into the golf club. Perhaps the afterlife was the same. They didn't want his sort making the place look untidy. He'd been blackballed out of heaven.

Then, one night, after a busy day trying to push a pencil off a desk, he felt a chill wind blow through the office. He turned to see a woman walking through the wall. She was beautiful. In his old life, Mike would've definitely made a pass at her if they'd met in a bar. They stared at each other until Mike thought someone should speak.

'Who are you?' he asked.

Silence.

He tried again. 'Are you Death?'

A smile. 'Sometimes.'

'Oh, okay. I thought you'd be more… y'know… grim.'

'I'm new.'

'Younger model, eh?'

'Something like that.'

'What happened to the old one?'

'We think he's retired. We're looking into it.' She stretched her fingers out, turning her hands over, a curious expression on her face. It seemed like she was experiencing her body for the first time. 'What are these called?'

'Fingers?'

'Oh. Right.' She nodded. 'And this thing I'm nodding?'

'Your head.'

'Fascinating. You must excuse me, I was only recently born into existence. I'm still learning the ropes. In fact, what are ropes?'

Mike harrumphed. At least he could still do that from beyond the grave. This wasn't the service he was used to. 'Is there someone in charge I could speak to? I've been hanging around here for ages with no information.'

46

'I assure you, I am the highest authority.' She took a step towards Mike, still wobbly on new legs. 'You should be honoured. You're my first.'

THE SECOND ATTEMPT travelling to Bethnal Green passed without incident or comment, and every other station on the route was where it was expected to be. Nobody said anything. It was too odd for anyone to verbalise. It surely couldn't have happened, and if nobody mentioned it, then it didn't.

When they reached his stop, Dave peeled himself away from the mass of humanity in the carriage and dropped onto the platform. His breath was ragged as the tunnel walls seemed to close in on him. He couldn't get to the surface quick enough, taking the escalator steps two at a time. He continued to run once he was on the streets, trying to put as much distance between him and the station as possible before his lungs burned and he staggered to a halt. There'd been a familiar sensation down in the tunnel; one he'd hoped he would never experience again.

He walked the rest of the way to Crow Road. Anne and Death already had the kettle on by the time he'd climbed the stairs to the office. He was about to tell them about his journey to work, but Death's chin covered with tiny pieces of toilet paper distracted him.

'I take it you tried shaving for the first time this morning?' he said. Death bristled.

'I think I did pretty well for someone who didn't even have a face until recently.'

'Fair enough. We've got bigger things to deal with,' replied Dave.

'What do you mean?'

'Have you ever had a hangover so bad it curved time and space?' Dave asked, before describing his journey to work and the minor matter of reality breaking down around him.

'It felt like when we were in the boardroom in UberSystems Tower,' he said when he'd finished.

'Do you think he's back?' asked Anne.

'Who? Conquest? I don't know. There's something going on, though. I think—'

The harsh blare of the door buzzer interrupted him. All three of them exchanged a quizzical glance. Anne walked over to the intercom and pressed the button.

'Yes?' she spoke into the microphone.

'It's the police,' a voice crackled in reply. Anne and Death exchanged more glances, this time of a less quizzical variety.

'How did they find you?' Anne asked.

Death shook his head. 'I don't know.'

'Just hide in your office. I'll get rid of them. You too, Dave.'

'Why me?'

'You look and smell like someone dragged through a hedge backwards by a pint of Guinness.'

'Fair point.'

Death ran to his office and collided with the door, rattling it in its frame. Anne sighed. It would be one of those days.

SAM RELEASED THE intercom button. There was a sigh from the speaker. 'Hold on. I'll come down.'

While he waited, Sam looked around Crow Road. The red brick buildings lining the cobblestoned road seemed more like the home of start-ups and warehouse apartments than an ancient crime-fighting society. He checked the address on the business card before pocketing it in his jacket.

Sam had stayed up most of the night looking through Alfred Graves's diaries. According to the entries, he'd worked many cases with the Gentlemen of Dubious Activities and had a good relationship with them. There were, as the name suggested, dubious activities along with events that sat on the end of the scale marked 'unusual'. Some people - Alfred Graves included - would say only the supernatural could explain a handful of those stories. Sam put this down to Victorian superstition.

His searches of the Police National Database for the group had returned no results, and Wikipedia had only told him there was a drinking club with that name in Toronto. So here he was, following in the footsteps of his ancestors. This is the reason he'd joined the police force. The thin blue —

An IC1 female, mid-thirties, dark hair, nice eyes, opened the door. Sam flashed his warrant card.

'DCI Graves. May I ask you a few questions?' The woman leant on the doorframe, blocking his way in.

'What sort of questions? I'm busy at the moment.'

'I'm trying to locate a group of individuals who call themselves the Gentlemen of Dubious Activities.' The woman straightened up at the mention of the name. Perhaps Sam might get somewhere with this lead.

'You'd better come in.' Sam followed her up the flight of stairs.

'And you are?' he asked as they climbed.

'Anne Mitchell,' Anne answered over her shoulder.

'This is a nice part of town. What do you do here?'

'We're a consultancy.'

'And what do you consult on?'

They reached the top of the stairs. Anne turned and smiled at him. 'Personnel matters.'

She led him into a small office furnished with two desks and some battered filing cabinets. A door with frosted glass led to a second room. The ceiling was low, and the carpet worn. Anne gestured towards a chair at the tidier of the two desks (she had considered tidying Dave's desk while he was away, but decided it might be better to discuss just torching the whole thing and starting again).

'Please, take a seat. Can I get you a drink?'

Sam sat down. 'No, thank you. So how many consultants work here?'

Anne took the chair on the opposite side of the desk. 'There's me, a junior consultant and the owner.'

Sam looked around the deserted office. 'Where's everyone else, then?'

'Dave, the junior member of staff, is on holiday and the owner is taking a sabbatical.'

'And what's his name?'

Anne clasped her hands on the desk. 'So, how can I help you? You mentioned something about some gentlemen doing dodgy jobs?'

'Dubious Activities,' Sam corrected her.

'Well, I assure you there's nothing dodgy or dubious going on here.' There was that smile again. Sam reached into his coat pocket and dropped the business card onto the desk.

'That's a shame, because they gave me this and told me I'd find them here.' It disappointed Sam to see the smile disappear. Anne shifted in her seat.

'Who's "they"?'

'My boss. Do you know them?'

'Your boss? Why would I know them?'

'No, the Gentlemen of Dubious Activities. You wouldn't want to know my boss.' Anne picked the card up and twirled it in her fingers, examining the raised white text against the black.

'The Gentlemen of Dubious Activities, you say? That's a name I've not heard in a long time.'

'So the group doesn't exist anymore?'

Anne shook her head. The surviving members disbanded in the early eighties.'

'*Surviving* members?'

'There was some unpleasantness in Russia. Not all of them made it back. We came along afterwards.'

'Does your organisation have a name?'

'No, we've not needed one. We don't advertise or anything.'

'And what's "personnel matters" a euphemism for?'

'I'm sorry, but what's this about?'

Sam took the card back. He considered whether he should continue this conversation. Collins had told him to track down the Gentlemen of Dubious Activities, but he'd hit a dead-end. An interesting new lead had revealed itself, though. What harm could it do to explore it? This Anne Mitchell had some knowledge of what he was talking about and could prove useful.

'I'm sure you're aware of what happened down at UberSystems Tower?'

Anne nodded. 'I've seen it on the news.'

'Yeah, well, I'm the poor sod they've asked to work out what's gone on.'

'And what's gone on?'

Sam shrugged. 'I have no idea, but this address came up in conversation and my boss suggested the GDA may help. So I wondered if you wanted to come with me and have a look around. Give your opinion?'

'I don't think I'll be any help. Anyway, I've far too much to do around here.'

'Look, I'm missing one rich white guy. That makes those on a higher pay grade than me nervous. My car's just downstairs. I promise I won't take up too much of your time. You don't seem rushed off your feet here.'

Anne's eyes darted towards the door to Death's office. Sam looked over his shoulder, following her glance. 'Is there something in there that you need to attend to?'

Anne looked down at the desk. 'No. I'll come. Let me get my coat.'

DEATH HUGGED THE floor. The floor was his friend. The floor did not move. Dave sat against the wall, his eyes closed, until they heard the front door slam.

Dave crawled on all fours to the office door and cracked it open.

'They've both gone.'

'What do we do now?' Death whispered.

'I don't know. Why are we still whispering?' Dave hissed back as his phone chimed. He looked at the screen. 'It's from Anne.'

'What's she said?'

'The cops aren't after you. They're investigating the whole Conquest and disappearing building debacle. She said not to worry and she'll be back as soon as she can.'

'So we're on our own?' Death asked, nervous.

'Yes.'

'Oh dear. That's never worked out well, has it?'

'Still, I'm not the one that wants to kill you,' said Dave with a shrug.

'I think that might be the only way to cure this hangover, but we can't even say if it'll work.'

'Are you scared?'

'Even in this short time I've learned that when you have a life; a finite period in which to get everything done, you're reluctant to give it up.'

'Yeah, but if it works you'll get out of that body. You can go back to being Death and transport yourself anywhere, be immortal, all that good stuff.'

'What if I don't want to?'

'But you're Death.'

'So? Why does that mean I'm fated to perform that task forever? Are humans restricted to one job for their entire lives?'

'Well, no, but—'

Death pushed himself up onto his elbows. 'Why am I the only one who doesn't get a choice? Anyone could do it. It's not like it's rocket science, or anything. You just need to wear a cloak and say, "Wooah. Just walk into the light, mate".'

'So what do you want to do with your life, then?'

'I don't know, but I think I'd like the chance to find out.'

'And what happens to everyone while you have this mid-eternity crisis?'

'Something will come up. It always does.'

'Okay. Let's start small. What are your plans for the rest of the day? Should we look into my train ride?'

'I'm not sure I'm in a condition to deal with a wonky space-time continuum. I want to be among you for a while. It's been too long since I've just walked along a street as life moved around me. Let's see the sights.'

'You must have seen them loads of times.'

'But it's not the same, Dave. This time, I'm here, I'm one of you. I matter. Hell, I *am* matter. You live in a universe for ages, but you never get round to doing the tourist-y things.'

Dave rose to his feet, clinging to the wall as he did so. 'I think I can manage that. What do you want to do first?'

'A cultural pilgrimage, I feel. I want to visit the home of one of my favourite fictional crime-fighting characters. Let's go to Baker Street.'

'Ah,' Dave said, nodding his head knowingly. 'Sherlock Holmes.'

'No. Danger Mouse.'

ANNE HAD NEVER been in a police car before and found it difficult to resist twisting all the knobs and dials until she found one that turned the lights and siren on. Luckily, there wasn't one labelled 'Make Car Go Woo-Woo'. She looked at DCI Graves out of the corner of her eye, letting her gaze linger. He was handsome in a buttoned-up sort of way. He probably looked good in a uniform, even with that hairy slug clinging to his top lip. Facial hair didn't convince Anne. As far as she was concerned, it was only suitable for Tom Selleck, Victorian engineers and identifying evil doppelgangers from parallel universes.

'So, what do you know about the GDA, which we appear to be calling it now?' she asked to break the silence they'd sat in for the duration of the journey. Sam's eyes didn't leave the road ahead.

'My great-great-grandfather was an officer in the Met and he worked with the original line-up. The force brought them in over the decades until the early eighties, when they dropped off the radar. I've not been able to find out anything about the various members over the years, only that they could solve unsolvable cases.'

'So you think this case is unsolvable?'

Sam turned his attention from the road to Anne. 'I don't think any case is unsolvable. Once you eliminate the impossible, whatever remains, no matter how batshit, must be the truth. My boss insisted I try to find them, but as they don't appear to be available, you'll do.'

Wow. Nice eyes. They diverted attention away from the moustache. Anne cleared her throat. 'So have the Graves always been police officers, then?'

Sam returned to concentrating on the road. 'It's the family business,' he replied with a thin smile.

'Are you going to give me a summary of the situation like they do on cop shows?'

'On the evening of the seventh of May, members of the public reported multiple disturbances throughout Greater London. The epicentre appeared to be the Canary Wharf area and UberSystems Tower, the head office of the multi-national corporation UberSystems International. At around seven o'clock, witnesses reported an intense white light shining from the windows, increasing in magnitude until it was too bright to look at.

'After several seconds, witnesses reporting hearing a loud rumble and the light receded, when, to quote one eyewitness, there was "sweet F.A. left" of the building, all its contents and - as far as we can determine - its sole occupant.'

'Conrad West?'

Sam nodded. 'Nobody's seen or heard from him since. He hasn't used his mobile phone, no ports of entry have flagged his passport, and what bank accounts we're aware of haven't been accessed. But a bloke like that has loads stashed away around the world and knows how to get his hands on a private plane.'

Despite her better judgment, Anne was being drawn into a mystery to which she knew the solution. So much for vowing never to return to UberSystems Tower. Dave once told her that everything seemed to lead back there and it looked like he was right.

'Was there anything where the building used to be?'

'Structural engineers have checked it out. All infrastructure leading up into the building from below the surface looked as if someone had sliced it through and the building picked up and carried off.'

A thought occurred to Anne, and it made her shift in her seat. 'Any CCTV footage?'

'Nothing from UberSystems Tower, obviously. That's wherever the building is. All footage from surrounding buildings and public property has proved inconclusive. They all white-out at the key moment. We're trying to piece together what happened in the moments leading up to the event. We've got guys going through the footage, but there are too many members of the public and we don't know what we're looking for.'

Anne gave a sigh of relief.

'Though,' Sam continued, 'some material from a building across the road came in so fingers crossed there's something in there. That information is just the greatest hits. If anything comes from this today, we'll provide you with a full briefing. So what do you think? Do you have a plan?'

Anne had no idea what she should be doing. Still, years in this business had taught her the finer points of winging it. 'I need to see the scene.'

'That won't be a problem. If you need anything just ask, Miss Mitchell.'

'Thank you. And call me Anne.' She saw the glimmer of a smile at the edge of DCI Graves's lips.

'I'm Sam.'

Anne noticed the traffic thin out as they approached UberSystems Plaza, former address of UberSystems International and location of UberSystems Tower. People were staying away for fear that they too might slip down the same rabbit hole. A chunk had been carved out of the skyline where the building once stood. As they drew closer, she couldn't help but think of a rotten tooth extraction.

Sam parked alongside two squad cars. He killed the engine and stepped out the Vauxhall Astra, followed by Anne. Nodding to the constable standing guard, he slid the bolt on the door in the tall wooden walls that ringed the site and opened the door for Anne, so she could see the plot for the first time. It was like watching footage of a building site being played in reverse. Fingers of twisted steel poked out from the sand used to cover up the broken foundations while engineers tackled thick power cables with chainsaws. Tractors and rollers circled around the perimeter, smoothing the edges, wiping away any remaining traces of what happened here.

The ground dropped away immediately beyond the door, so Sam and Anne carefully stepped onto the site floor.

'Is the car park still underneath?' Anne asked, walking across the flat expanse.

'Yeah, several cars had been vandalised. We examined them, but found nothing.'

Anne stopped in her tracks. 'Did you feel that?'

'What?' asked Sam. Anne crouched down, placed an open hand on the mud.

'There! A humming.' Sam followed her lead, his palm pressed into the wet topsoil. The vibration travelled up his arm and into his chest.

'It's probably just a tube train. The Jubilee line passes right underneath.'

Anne knew this had nothing to do with public transport. A wave of emotion threatened to pull her under, as it had on the top floor of UberSystems Tower. It seemed to be coming out of the ground itself. But Dave had banished it, hadn't he?

Beneath her fingers there were tectonic shifts in the fabric of the universe. Circular waves radiated through the surrounding dirt, the pebbles and stones leapfrogging each other with a steady rhythm.

'Actually,' Sam said. 'This doesn't feel like a—'

Before he could finish the sentence, reality hiccuped and Anne and Sam winked out of existence…

'CAMERA?'
    'Check.'
    'Wallet?'
    'Check.'
    'Suntan lotion. You're not used to having skin. We don't want you to burn.'
    'Check.'
    'Keys?'
    'Nope.'
    'Where are your keys?'
    Death shrugged. 'I've had no use for keys. It's one perk of being able to transport instantly to any location.'
    'But what if you're working late and have to lock up?' Dave asked. Death laughed.
    'I don't understand this concept of "working late" of which you speak.'
    Not being the most organised of duos, Death and Dave were still preparing to leave the office. Death had been placing the items Dave called out into a bum bag[1] he'd found in a cupboard and strapped around his waist. Style was timeless, after all.
    'Here they are,' Dave said, pulling a set of keys from a desk drawer. 'Let's go.'

THE ALARM IN the control room burst into life, its teeth-grating wail making Carroll drop the stack of

---

[1] Note to American readers: A 'bum bag' is what you would call a 'fanny pack', but in British English 'fanny' is a word too rude to publish in a respectable comedy-fantasy novel. Oh, bugger.

spreadsheets he was holding. He didn't know they'd had an alarm installed.

'What the bloody hell is that?' he yelled over the din.

'Power surge,' shouted a technician whose name Carroll couldn't quite remember. It was Fred or Frank.

'Where?'

Fredorfrank punched some buttons on a keyboard and brought up a map of the area on the monitor in front of him. After some study, he tapped the screen with a finger and said, 'Ground Zero. Surface level.'

'Can we get eyes on it?'

Fredorfrank clicked the mouse, and the image changed. The square of land upon which UberSystems Tower used to stand. Two tractors trundled around. Nothing of any interest.

'Back it up,' Carroll barked as if he was in a poor quality cop show. The footage rewound and, after a second or so, two figures - a man and a woman - appeared in the centre of the screen. 'Play it.'

The room gathered around the monitor and watched the couple walk across the site and drop to their knees. Then, without warning, they disappeared in a flash of light.

The good mood Carroll had been feeling since yesterday's successful test evaporated. He assumed the vanishing act was part of the ongoing police investigation. He'd asked for a good, old-fashioned cover-up, but the Permanent Secretary had assured him the inquiry would be closed as quickly as they had opened it. 'What just happened?'

Fredorfrank was making his way through the numbers. 'The initial indications are a temporary wormhole opened up where they stood, then collapsed. That entire area is unstable. Nobody should walk around there like that.'

'A wormhole? Do we know where they've ended up.'

'I shouldn't worry,' assured Fredorfrank. 'The data's showing it was localised. It would've just dropped them off down the road.'

Caroll rolled his eyes. 'Well, that should be all right, then.' He took a breath. 'I want a briefing with every team leader in the conference room in two hours. Full root cause analysis. How'd this happen? Where did they end up? What's the probability this will reoccur? Where's the military liaison?'

A stern-looking man in an army officer's uniform marched up. 'Yes, sir?'

'Excellent, Captain Mills. Gather the footage from all the cameras on-site. I want those two identified, found and brought in as soon as possible.'

Mills gave a short, efficient nod and marched off to find someone to shout at.

'What does this mean for the minister's visit later on?' a junior technician asked.

'It means nothing at all. The demonstration will go ahead as planned.' Caroll clapped his hands. 'Now, everybody get moving.'

Now their tasks distracted his staff, Caroll slumped into the nearest chair to have a proper wallow in misery. This was just his luck. Mere hours from the culmination of his life's work and people were looking to screw the whole thing up by vanishing into other realms. It was so rude.

He couldn't postpone the minister's visit. She was already doubtful of the entire enterprise and would grasp any opportunity to cancel what she suspected was an expensive folly. Better to invest the money in bullets and bombs. You knew where you stood with those.

Caroll pulled himself to his feet. He would keep his dream alive. He wouldn't let a minor matter like two members of public vanishing down a wormhole hold him back.

'Somebody get me a coffee,' he shouted above the chatter. 'And I want that exit point calculated now!'

... AND UNREALITY SPAT Anne and Sam back out.

Sam collapsed and crashed onto a cold stone floor, his senses scattered. He rolled over onto his back and slowly opened his eyes, expecting to be welcomed into the afterlife. Though his vision was blurred, he could just make out a serene light filtering down through a curved glass roof, beneath which the recently departed ascended on escalators. A nice concession to modern living, Sam thought. Suddenly, the air crackled with anticipation. An important message was to come down from on high.

'Passengers are reminded to keep their items with them at all times. Unattended items can cause delays and may be removed and destroyed.'

Sam pushed himself up onto his elbows to see Anne already on her feet. He looked around and recognised his surroundings as the concourse of Canary Wharf underground train station, which was half a mile away from where they'd been only a few seconds ago. Commuters swerved around them as if pushed by a force field made up of the Urge-Not-to-Get-Involved.

Sam clambered to his feet, trying to keep an air of cool, but his head span and he staggered around. 'What the bloody hell happened?'

'My best guess is a wormhole,' Anne replied, dusting herself off.

Sam looked at her blankly.

'An interdimensional portal linking two points in space.'

Still a blank look.

Anne took Sam gently by the arm. 'Come on. Let's get you a drink.'

DAVE AND DEATH took the tube across London and, before long, they stood on Baker Street, home to Sherlock Holmes, at least two crime-fighting rodents and a legendary saxophone riff. It was a street of two halves; three lanes of one-way traffic flanked on one side by elegant Georgian townhouses, with tee shirt shops and ice cream parlours on the other. Death stopped outside a newsagent selling souvenirs.

'Let's get a postcard,' he said, picking a picture of Buckingham Palace from a spinning rack outside the shop's entrance.

'Why? Who would you send it to? Everybody you know lives within a five-mile radius.'

'That's what you do, isn't it? You get a postcard, or one of those shirts with "I heart London" on it.'

'Only if I can buy one that says "I'm with stupid". Now, come on. I want to beat the crowds.'

Dave and Death joined the handful of people waiting for the lights to change at the crossing by the station exit. The traffic flowed smoothly, lighter now the rush hour was over. Death tapped his feet, impatient to get to the other side. He looked down to see a small child, a male of the variety as far as he could tell, who was staring back up at him. Death smiled politely. The child continued to stare back. Death decided to tell him a joke. Children liked jokes.

'Why did the chicken cross the road?' he asked.

'I don't know,' replied the child.

'To get to the idiot's house.'

'Oh.'

'Knock, knock,' Death continued.

'Who's there?' the child answered.

'The chicken.'

The child cried. Death took a step to the side, hoping its parent or owner hadn't noticed.

The traffic lights at the top of Baker Street changed to green and the waiting vehicles sped up, trying to get down the road before the set of lights Dave and Death stood at turned to red. They were too slow and decelerated as the pedestrians, including Death, stepped onto the road. One BMW driver, though, was caught up in the race and noticed the lights too late. He hit the brakes, causing the car to veer haphazardly across the tarmac and scrape the Ford in the next lane, cleanly removing its wing-mirror. Pedestrians scattered in all directions, apart from the small child who stared transfixed at the approaching vehicle. Death knew he should save this boy's life but he *had* been critical of his joke. The child had so much of his time ahead of him, it seemed churlish to allow it to be cut short. Perhaps, over the years, he could learn to appreciate humour. But this selfless act might kill Death, and he'd got rather attached to life, though this body had already seen a lot more of it than the kid. With only a fraction of a second to think, Death weighed up the pros and cons of the situation and then threw himself in front of the car, pushing the boy to safety. Death stood in the middle of the road, his eyes closed, waiting for the inevitable. The car skidded to a halt and gently nudged Death's groin. The entire street, pedestrians and traffic, froze for a moment before people ran to help.

Death was happy to see the young boy was unharmed. He stood up and pointed a finger at Death, his bottom lip wobbling. 'Mum! That man pushed me!'

Death learned then that he really didn't like kids.

ANNE DRAGGED SAM into a bar across the way from the station exit, shoved him into a corner, and put a drink in his hand. He calmed the shakes long enough to take a sip.

'What's your expert opinion on what happened, then?'

Anne ripped open the packet of pork scratchings she'd bought and pushed them across the table. 'UberSystems Tower didn't implode, or explode, or get carried away bit by bit by pixies. It's still in one piece, we're just not sure in which dimension. You rip something that large out of the universe, it'll leave a wound stuff can fall into.'

'So we're in another dimension?' asked Sam, helping himself to a scratching.

'No, but we took a shortcut through one.'

Sam burst out laughing. The idea Anne had voiced was so ludicrous, it was the only rational reaction. 'We just travelled through another dimension? You should warn me next time so I can take some photos.'

Anne took a sip of her drink and sat back. 'What do you think happened?'

Sam considered the options, then said, 'We walked over to the station, I slipped over and banged my head. I'm suffering a brief period of short-term memory loss and you've decided to wind me up.'

Anne shrugged. 'That's pretty good, but I assure you we travelled through a wormhole.'

'We did not teleport. There's no such thing.'

'You're right, we didn't teleport,' Anne replied.

'Ha! See? I knew you'd crack!' Sam cried out.

'Teleportation and travelling through wormholes are two very different things.'

Sam could feel his grip on sanity loosening. He buried his head in his hands and remembered a relaxation technique he'd read about in one of HR's health and well-being emails. He took a couple of deep breaths. Calmer, he looked back up at Anne. 'Thank you for helping with our inquiries, Ms Mitchell. I shall now escort you back to my vehicle and will return you to the location of our meeting, or to your place of residence, whichever is more convenient for you.'

Anne smiled. 'Well, let's at least finish our drinks.'

Sam's phone rang. He fished it out of his pocket and saw it was Kelvin calling. 'Excuse me, I need to take this. It's my sergeant.' Sam got up from the table as he answered the phone. 'Hello?'

'Hello, guv,' Kelvin replied. 'We've reviewed that CCTV footage they sent over.'

Sam headed for the exit, stepping out into the street. 'Yeah? Any good?'

'Three people of interest leaving the building a couple of minutes before the incident.' The investigation team hadn't settled on a term for what happened to UberSystems Tower.

Sam punched the air. 'Yes!'

'I've sent an image over.'

'Does that mean I have to look at my emails?' Sam asked with dread.

'I'm afraid it does, guv.'

Sam sighed. 'Give me a minute.'

He took the phone from his ear and opened his emails, ignoring the number that was approaching five digits. He found Kelvin's email between a polite request to keep the staff kitchen tidy and an invitation to leaving drinks for someone he'd never heard of. There was a picture attached and, though the image was grainy, Anne was recognisable leading a male and another female from the building. He took a deep breath and returned to the phone call.

'Send a squad car to the Barrow and Banker on Canada Square. I'm with one of them now.'

'Bloody hell, guv. You're good.'

'Yes, it seems I am.' Sam terminated the call and dropped the phone back into his jacket pocket. Anger bubbled up from his gut. She'd been playing him for a fool under the guise of helping with the case. He needed to go back inside, but what would his next step be? He couldn't arrest her. What would he charge her with? Conspiracy to hide a building? A polite invitation to come down to the station and answer a few questions would be the best approach.

He went back into the bar and walked up to the table as nonchalantly as he could.

'Everything alright?' Anne asked as he sat down.

'Can I ask where you were on the night of the seventh, Ms Mitchell?'

'Are we back to the formalities?' Anne asked, concerned.

'I'd just like you to answer the question.'

Anne realised something had happened on that phone call, something implicating her in this. Should she make a run for it? That was no use. There'd be other officers on their way. Even if she got away, Graves knew where she worked and probably where she lived. It would be best to play it cool. What could they charge her with? Possession of a flaming sword? Then she remembered not to mention the flaming sword.

'I don't remember,' Anne replied, coolly.

'Perhaps this will jog your memory.' He took the phone out of his pocket and placed it on the table with a flourish. This was the big *gotcha!* moment.

'The Crystal Palace squad? I know I wasn't with them.'

Sam looked down at the lock screen of his phone. 'Hang on. That's not right.' He picked the phone up and searched through his emails. 'Where's that gone then?'

'What are you looking for?'

'An email Sergeant Kelvin just sent me.'

'Have you looked in the deleted items?'

'Where's that, then?' Anne looked over.

'Go back. No, go *back.*'

'How do I do that?' Sam asked, flustered.

'Press "mailboxes". Now scroll down. Press on where it says "Trash".'

'There it is. Thanks.' Sam brought the picture back up and placed the phone back on the table with less of a flourish than before.

'Perhaps this will jog your memory,' he repeated, but he knew deep down the moment had passed. Anne looked at the black and white image.

'That makes more sense.'

The bar door swung open and two uniformed police officers entered. They saw Sam and walked over to the table, flanking Anne on either side. All eyes were on the drama playing out at table 12.

'I'd appreciate it if you'd come down to the station and answer a few questions,' Sam asked with a polite smile. Anne looked up at the reinforcements and realised they had trapped her. She drank what remained of her vodka and tonic in one gulp.

'Well, I had nothing planned for the rest of the afternoon.'

'LOOK AT WHAT you've done to my car!'

'What *I've* done? If you hadn't been driving like an idiot—'

'*Me* driving like an idiot? What about you coming around that corner like you're Ayrton Senna?'

This had been going on for half an hour now. There'd been a head-on collision on a country road. Both cars were right-offs and so were the drivers.

They continued to argue over blame as the fire brigade cut away the twisted metal around them.

What does it matter? She thought as she sat down on the kerb. She wasn't worried about her trousers getting dirty from the rain-soaked pavement. The universe would take care of that.

If She'd learned anything on her first morning on Earth, it was that humans were very hard work. They were all so angry. Yes, they'd reached a major milestone in life, but it's not like they didn't know it would happen. Human existence was a one-way ticket to a destination regularly signposted along the route.

The argument intensified when one driver tried to push the other. The problem with that, when you're two non-corporeal beings, is that it just results in a lot of stumbling and cursing. She would need to step in.

'Excuse me, gentlemen.'

They ignored her and continued to row. She coughed politely.

'Gentlemen, please.'

It was as if She wasn't there. Time for her outdoor voice. Summoning echoes of the screams rattling around the depths of Hell, she spoke slowly and clearly.

'Stop this.'

The command was like nails scratched down the motorists' souls. They did as She ordered them, their attention now focused on her.

'Sorry, we didn't notice you there,' the older of the two said sheepishly. She stood up, straightened her jacket.

'Evidently.'

'Is this the afterlife?' asked the younger one.

'I'm afraid so.' The two men hung their heads in sorrow. Then the older one looked up.

'Did you see the accident?'

'I see all.'

'Whose fault was it? His?'

She waved a hand and an ethereal glow consumed the two figures in front of her. Urgh. Men. They always have to be right.

She needed guidance. She couldn't be expected to be thrown in at the deep end and figure these people out all by herself. Just when She thought she'd grasped one aspect of them, the next person did the exact opposite to what she expected. The whole thing was baffling.

There it was again. A slight tug, as if She was attached to a rope pulling her to the next soul. It was never-ending.

She needed help, and She knew where to find it.

DEATH LAY ON a trolley in an Accident and Emergency department cubicle.

'These places are amazing,' he said to Dave, who was sitting on a chair in the corner. Dave, reading a pamphlet on knee injuries, nodded along absent-mindedly. 'Entire factories entirely dedicated to stopping people from dying. They come in broken one end and sent out the other, all bandaged and stitched up, kept from falling apart.'

A police car and ambulance had arrived on Baker Street quickly. While the police had worked to clear the streets and take statements, a paramedic named Laura checked on Death as he sat on the kerb outside an Italian chain restaurant.

'I think we should take you in and get you looked at properly,' Laura said, inspecting Death's head for any signs of trauma. 'You never know with this kind of thing. What seems like a light blow now could have caused some internal damage.'

'But I've got things I need to do,' Death said.

69

'It's better to be safe than sorry,' Laura replied. 'You don't want to be walking down the street in a couple of days and have your head fall off, do you?'

Death thought that sounded pretty cool, but muttered, 'No.'

'You really threw yourself in front of an oncoming vehicle to save a child?' Laura asked.

'Yes.' Death nodded, his head remaining attached to his neck.

'Wow,' Laura murmured, impressed. 'Right, what's your full name, Steve?'

Dave peered over the top of the pamphlet. 'Steve Newman? New man? That's the best name you could come up with?'

Death shrugged. 'I panicked.'

'And what are you doing chucking yourself in front of cars to save people? That's not a smart use of your body.'

'You can't throw any stones in that particular glass house,' Death answered back. 'You doing that is how we met!'

'And I would say doing that is a terrible idea.' Dave returned to reading about anterior cruciate ligament tears.

Death knew Dave was right. He was flesh and bone now, and if anybody knew how fragile a human body was, it was him. He had to be careful and take care of this vessel he found himself poured into. This was the only one he'd get.

'Knock, knock,' a voice said from behind the curtain.

'Come in,' Death called. The curtain rattled open and a familiar face appeared on the other side. Death sat up on his elbows. 'Emma?'

Emma glanced down at the clipboard in her hand. 'Hello, again. You're Steven Newman? Nice bum bag.'

Dave dropped the pamphlet onto his lap. 'Do you two know each other?'

'Emma helped me when I got lost here yesterday,' Death explained.

'Hello, Emma,' Dave said with a wave. 'I'm Dave.'

'Hi, Dave.' Emma waved back. 'What's your relationship with Steven here?'

'Just an interested party.'

'Ignore him,' Death said. 'He gets antsy if it's not him launching himself into the road and being the centre of attention. He's a friend.'

'Yes, I heard what you'd been up to,' said Emma. 'I'm not sure if it was brave or foolish.'

'In my experience, there's negligible difference between the two,' Death replied.

'Either way, as a medical professional, I really don't advise throwing yourself in front of traffic.'

'I'll make a note of that. Dave, write that down,' Death said. 'How's the small human? Did they bring him in here, too?'

'He's fine, thanks to you. Are you okay to sit up a bit?' Emma replied. Death shuffled his way up the bed until he was in a seated position.

'I'm going to give you a quick check-up, if that's all right with you?' Emma said, slipping on a pair of latex gloves.

'Absolutely fine,' replied Death.

'Are you in any pain at the moment?'

Death pointed at Dave. 'Well, he won't stop talking, but apart from that, no.'

Emma laughed and took a small pen torch from her tunic. 'I'm just going to examine your eyes, so if you can stare straight ahead for me.'

Emma took a step forward, bending down close enough to Death that he could feel her warm breath against his cheeks. He'd never been this close to a human before, never experienced the concept of

71

personal space until now. The beam of light flooded his vision, and, after a moment, Death felt her body weight shift as she moved to his other eye. There was a mixture of unease and intimacy in the way the two bodies curved around each other.

'So, where did this happen?' Emma asked, her voice in Death's ear. He swallowed, nervous for a reason he couldn't put his finger on.

'Baker Street.'

'What's over on Baker Street?'

'Well, there's a postbox there…' Death realised how idiotic this sounded.

'Oh, Danger Mouse? I've always meant to see it, but that's the problem when you live in the city. You never go to the sights unless someone visits.'

'That's what I said.'

Emma stood up straight and dropped the torch back into her pocket. 'That all looks good. Are you experiencing any nausea?'

'Some, but I think that's just the beer I drank last night.'

Emma held a finger up. 'I want you to follow my finger with your eyes. Don't move your head.'

'This isn't a sobriety test, is it? Because I assure you, my headache confirms I'm past being drunk and well into the hangover stage.'

'Can I ask you a question?' Emma said, her finger bouncing around Death's field of vision like an enemy spaceship in an 80s video game. Death sighed.

'Fine, but I think they should teach you this at nursing school. When a mummy and daddy love each other very much they get certain urges—'

'No, not that,' Emma interrupted. 'I wanted to ask, why did you do what you did? Was it a conscious decision, or instinct?'

Death shrugged. 'It was the right thing to do. Isn't that what humans should strive for? Though, in my experience, not nearly enough of you do. Don't get me wrong, I can understand why, and it's not my job to judge. It's hard doing the right thing. I've learned that today. You just need to be kinder. Extra-terrestrial lifeforms won't reveal themselves until you stop being wankers to each other. They were very specific about it the last time we spoke.'

Emma smiled, folded her arms. 'Has anyone ever told you you're a bit odd?'

'Is that your medical opinion?'

'Just an observation. That's cool, though. I like odd.'

Emma finished her examination and confirmed that, physically at least, Death was fine.

'You're free to go,' she told him, 'but be careful. I don't want to hear you've been washed out to sea trying to get to Fraggle Rock.'

'I'M TELLING YOU, she was interested. And I know you liked her,' Dave said, leaning back in his desk chair. After Death had been discharged from the hospital, he didn't feel in the mood to revisit the scene of his accident so they returned to Crow Road.

'How could you tell?' Death asked.

'You were showing off, which is what people do when they're not smart enough to be interesting. I'm speaking from experience. What did it feel like when you saw her?'

'I felt sick, but a happy sick if that makes any sense?'

Dave nodded. 'You should've asked for her number.'

'I'm not sure I'm ready for that.'

'Look, you said you want to try on being human. This is part of being human.'

'What if she said "no"? I get the sense that would be worse than not knowing how she felt.'

Dave shrugged. 'Sometimes you just have to take a leap of faith.'

'Yeah, well, what you gonna do about it?'

'I dunno. Do you want to look into what happened to me this morning?'

'Your train looping back on itself on a straight track?'

'We need to investigate.'

Death sat up in his chair. 'Why do we?'

'Because that's what we do.'

'Is it? We're just two ordinary blokes now. There's enough for us to sort out at the moment,' Death said, pointing at his own face. 'Let it be somebody else's problem for once.'

The buzzer for the front door sounded. Dave sighed. 'I'll get that. We'll continue this conversation when I get back.'

Dave went down the stairs and answered the door. A beautiful, confused-looking woman dressed all in black stood on the doorstep. Dave assumed she was lost because women who looked like that didn't call at doors that Dave would be behind.

'Can I help?' he asked.

'Are you Death?'

'I certainly feel like it,' Dave quipped before he'd registered what the woman had asked. She looked him up and down.

'You're not what I had in mind.'

'I'm sorry?' Dave said. 'Who did you ask for?'

'Death.'

'Yeah, that's what I thought you said. Nobody with that name lives here. Death living in London? What a preposterous idea.' Dave leaned forward, beyond the doorframe and looked down Crow Road. No-one was there. The woman tilted her head.

'Ah! These are one of those things you humans call a lie.' She was catching on. Dave straightened up.

'I'm not lying.'

'Your breathing pattern has altered, your heart rate has increased and your pupils have dilated.'

'Have you been taking lessons from my mum?'

'I take it they're inside?' The woman barged past Dave and marched up the stairs.

'Hey!' Dave yelled. 'You can't come in here!'

The woman gave Dave a look that would allow her to go pretty much wherever the hell she wanted. She continued up the stairs until she reached the small landing. There, Death was trying to squeeze a packet of digestives into his bum bag, which he still hadn't taken off. When he looked up and saw the visitor stood in the door frame, he dropped the packet to the floor. He cleared his throat.

'I wondered if you might show up.'

DEATH STARED AT the young woman sitting on the other side of his desk, unsure of what to say. Her eyes darted around the room, inquisitive, absorbing information, until they fixed on the door as Dave blundered through carrying a tray of tea and biscuits.

'So, do you have a name?' Death asked her. She shrugged.

'How about Death 2: Electric Boogaloo?' Dave suggested as he passed out mugs of tea and a plate piled high with chocolate Hobnobs. 'We could call you Classic Death.'

'Can I carry on being Steve Newman? I'm getting rather attached to it. She's Death now.'

'Okay, Steve,' Dave said, rolling his eyes. With that simple word, the taking of a human name, his life as Death ended and his human existence was fully born. 'But *she's* not a Death. You were a Death, a Grim Reaper. She's decidedly not grim. She's more like an angel.'

'Azrael is traditionally the name of the Angel of Death,' said Death

'If that's what you feel is appropriate, then I shall call myself Azrael,' Azrael said. She looked at the contents of the mug with apprehension. 'Should we be drinking something that's brown? That doesn't seem wise.'

'Where did you come from?' Dave asked, dipping a biscuit into his tea until the chocolate had melted.

'I was called into being,' Azrael replied.

'I think I understand,' said Death. 'The universe is exquisitely balanced. All things must have their opposite. Light and dark. Good and evil. Chocolate Bourbons and Custard Creams. When I ended up in this body and could not perform my duties, Life no longer had its converse concept. The universe needed to fill the gap and so this new Death - Azrael - was born.'

'Seems legit,' Dave said. 'But why does she look like she does and you looked like - well - you did?'

Death looked over at Azrael to see if she had an answer. When she had none, he said, 'I think the universe is accommodating for modern tastes. Everyone expects the famous to be young and beautiful, and you get no more famous than Death.'

'What were you like before?' Azrael asked Death, curiosity crossing her brow. Dave pulled up a picture on his phone and showed it to her. She nodded. 'The scythe is a nice touch.'

Dave considered things for a moment. 'So does that mean you can't turn back? Then there'd be two Deaths, and that doesn't sound great.'

'I hadn't thought about that.' Death lapsed into silence, then asked, 'How did you find me?'

'You still have an aura. I can see it half a world away. It's shrinking, though. Soon it will be gone.'

'Why did you come here? I'm an ordinary man now, it seems.'

'I need help. Teach me.'

'Teach you what?'

'How to deal with these humans. They're angry and annoying. They never listen and are petty, even when shown how much bigger the universe is than they are.'

Dave nodded in agreement. 'Yep, sounds like us.'

'Let me get this straight,' said Death. 'You want me to be your tutor?'

Azrael looked around the office. 'You don't seem that busy.'

Death shrugged. 'Yeah, fair enough.'

'No Danger Mouse, then?' Dave asked, disappointment in his voice.

'I'm sorry, but not today. No.'

'What's a mouse and why is it dangerous?' asked Azrael.

LORRAINE ARDEN MP, the Minister of Defence, barrelled around the spiral staircase that led down to the control room of Project Sisko. It was more compact than she had imagined, so at least there was a cost saving there between fantasy and reality. Dr Carroll was waiting for her at the foot of the stairs. The minister didn't suffer fools gladly, so she soon realised her career choice as a politician was a grave mistake. Despite his qualifications and degrees, she thought the scientist a buffoon; an 'educated idiot' as her grandfather called them.

Carroll buried his nerves as deep as he could. Though they'd been unable to find the two figures involved in the earlier power surge, the team had assured him that the chances of it reoccurring were very low.

'Thank you for coming, Minister,' he said with an anxious smile. Arden ignored his extended hand.

'Let's just get on with this, shall we, Doctor? I've three more of these to visit today before I have a meeting with the prime minister.' She marched past the computer banks, Carroll following behind like an obedient puppy trying to please its owner. The research assistants and technicians sat at their stations, silent, staring straight ahead. She peered through the window at the front of the room. 'What's this one again? Temporal distortions?'

'No, ma'am. We're interdimensional pathways. We opened gateways between worlds at the UberSystems site and we're studying ways to navigate through them, remember?'

'And what use is that to me?' Arden asked, like a school teacher asking for a pupil's workings.

'One practical application would be wormholes. Current theory is we'd be able to take shortcuts through other dimensions. When mapped properly, you'd be able to travel from one point to another instantly.'

'What else?'

Carroll thought that was pretty good on its own, but he continued. 'There could be infinite new worlds to explore out there. New resources, new technologies.'

'New dangers, you mean.'

'The possibilities are endless,' Carroll replied, concluding the minister was a glass-half-empty kind of person.

'What are we doing today?'

Carroll signalled a technician on the front row of desks, who pressed a button on his keyboard. This alerted someone on the other side of the shielded door leading to the laboratory beyond the glass. It swung open and a white-coated engineer carrying a bowl of peonies walked in.

They'd placed two empty plinths in the centre of the room and the engineer placed the bowl on one of them, nodded to his audience in the control room, and left.

'We'll instantaneously move that bowl of flowers from that plinth to one on the other side of the room. This a preliminary test with the aim of transporting them over a much larger distance.'

'Interflora must be shitting themselves,' the minister muttered under her breath.

'I know it seems trivial, but we need to carry the tests out on organic matter. Plus, they make the room look pretty.'

'Let's get on with it, then.'

Carroll pointed to an empty chair. 'Please, take a seat and we'll get started.'

Arden sat down and started checking the messages on her phone. Carroll was no longer worried. In two minutes he would blow her mind with the combination of physics and horticulture. All the calculations had been checked and double-checked. The events of earlier that day were an aberration.

'Begin the procedure,' Carroll ordered the room, kick-starting a flurry of activity. They had installed a large red LED timer above the window and it counted down from ten. It did nothing practical, but Carroll thought it would lend the whole procedure an air of drama.

'We're just powering up the Thingummy, which is used to stabilise the connection between dimensions,' Carroll explained to Arden, who appeared to be playing some kind of farming game on her phone.

Eight.

The low-level hum of chatter that usually permeated the control room died away.

Seven.

Data swamped the computer monitors as the code started with millisecond accuracy.

Six.

The device between the two plinths spluttered into life and a soft whine filled the gaps where the scientists' conversation had been until recently.

Five.

The minister of defence won enough money to purchase more grain for her chickens.

Four.

The disappointingly familiar clamour of the alarm shattered Carroll's hopes. Arden looked up from her phone and noticed the timer had stopped its countdown.

'What's going on?'

Carroll responded with a tight smile. 'Let me just check.'

He walked over to Dr Rose's workstation, giving a good impression of remaining calm even though his legs were shaking. 'What the bloody hell is going on?' he hissed.

Rose scanned the read-outs with a well-practiced eye. 'Something's wrong.'

'Really? Because I thought that was the good news alarm going off.'

'There's no need to get snippy.' Rose's fingers danced over the keyboard as she searched out the pieces of code that would help her. She stopped, tapped the screen with a finger. 'Here we are. Another energy surge.'

'Can you pinpoint the location?' Carroll asked through gritted teeth as he gave a thumbs-up to the minister.

'Is everything okay?' she asked. Carroll waved away her concerns.

'Perfectly fine. Just a few teething troubles, which is understandable on a project of this size.'

'Got it!' Rose shouted triumphantly.

'Where?' Rose had brought a schematic of the infrastructure below ground.

'Directly below Ground Zero. It looks like it was in one of the Jubilee line tunnels.'

Carroll gave a sigh of relief. 'Well, at least there was nobody around this time. Okay, let's get this show back on the road.'

Carroll turned round to find a technician waving a phone in his face. 'It's Captain Mills, Doctor. He says it's urgent.'

Carroll sighed and snatched the phone. More fires to fight, no doubt. 'You'd better be quick,' he spat into the receiver.

'We have non-optimal scenario,' Mills replied.

'What does that mean?'

'We've picked up some chatter on the Transport for London radio channels.'

'And?'

'They're saying they're light one Jubilee line train carriage.'

'Fascinating. How do their poor logistics affect me?'

'Well, it was between two other train carriages and travelling beneath Ground Zero when it disappeared.'

Carroll took some time to process that information before saying the only thing that came to mind.

'Bugger.'

ANNE CHECKED HER watch. The cup of coffee they'd given her when she arrived at the police station had gone cold on the table in front of her. The interview room was painted in that shade of government blue invented in a lab in the 1970s to break spirits and crush dissent. Posters urged the reader to keep an eye out for crime, and the carpet on which she nervously stamped her feet was threadbare grey. She shifted uncomfortably on a chair apparently designed by someone who'd only heard about spines once in a passing comment. The security camera tucked up in a corner of the ceiling gazed at her oppressively, the blinking red light a constant reminder that someone was watching behind the lens.

The door opened and Sam entered carrying a cardboard folder, followed by a younger man in a cheaper suit. They sat easily on the other side of the table, their spines conditioned to the chairs. Sam placed the folder on the table and gave his most professional smile. 'I'm sorry to have kept you waiting, Ms Mitchell,' he said. 'This is my colleague Detective Sergeant Kelvin who's assisting me with this investigation. Before we start, I'd like to remind you we're treating you as a witness and you're not under caution.'

Anne mirrored the police officer's smile. 'Just a friendly chat, then?'

'Exactly.' Sam opened the folder and slid a copy of the CCTV image out. There she was. Anne, along with Dave and Melanie, running out of the revolving doors of UberSystems Tower. They'd got her bang to rights, or whatever it was coppers on the telly said. Sam sat quietly for a moment, letting the photograph do the work, then sat forward, his hands clenched on the table. 'So, in the spirit of amiable chit-chat, what were you and your friends doing leaving UberSystems Tower mere minutes before it disappeared?'

Anne sat back in her chair, trying to display an air of calm, but that just made her back spasm so she hunched forward again. She weighed up her options. She'd rather not tell them anything at all, but she had to give them something. If she told them the truth, the worst-case scenario would be that they thought she was crazy. Time to go big or go home. Anne fixed Sam with a steely glare.

'The angry spirits of a suicide cult possessed UberSystems Tower, and it was their dark power that consumed the city and caused the violence you saw.'

Anne could see Sam trying to re-group behind his eyes. 'You mean "haunted", don't you?' Kelvin asked, trying to fill the silence.

'Sorry?'

'You said the building was possessed by ghosts, but buildings are haunted, aren't they?'

'No, these were buried in the infrastructure down to the foundations. They were part of the building itself.' Anne pointed to Dave in the photograph. 'That's why, when this guy exorcised them, they pulled UberSystems Tower with them.'

Sam and his sergeant looked at each other. There was an almost imperceptible shrug of Sam's shoulders that said 'go with it'.

'So you don't know what happened to the building?' asked Kelvin.

'We don't know where the dead go when they cross over, but we think it's some other plane of reality.'

'How does Conrad West fit into this?' asked Sam.

'He commissioned UberSystems Tower's construction to channel the spirits' energy. As far as I'm aware, he remained on the top floor when it all happened. The captain went down with the boat.'

'Ship,' corrected Kelvin. 'The captain went down with his ship.'

'What's the difference?' Sam asked, confused.

'Well, that's a bone of contention among the sailing community. Some say a ship is a vessel that has two or more continuous decks above sea level, other say that it's simply any vessel that can carry a boat.'

Sam shook his head and sighed. 'Truly every day is a school day working with you Kelvin.' He turned back to Anne. 'I don't understand why Mr West wanted to build a skyscraper full of ghosts? It doesn't seem to be the most practical approach from an interior design point of view.'

Anne shrugged. 'I'm not clear on that part, either. I wasn't really paying attention.'

'So, all this time, we've been looking on the wrong… What did you call it?' Sam grasped for the right word.

'Plane of reality?' suggested Kelvin. Sam snapped his fingers.

'That's it, Kelvin. I knew there was a reason I kept you around. That and the boat stuff. So all the evidence is no longer on this plane of reality and we just have to take your word for it? That's all rather convenient, isn't it?'

'I can assure you a missing building is not convenient in any way.'

Sam opened and closed his mouth, unsure of what to say. Police work became a lot more complicated when you included more than the standard three dimensions. He took a fresh approach. He planted a finger on the photograph, pointing to Dave.

'Who's this then? Some kind of priest?'

Anne laughed. 'No, he's not any kind of priest.'

'But you said he performed exorcisms. That's usually in their job description.'

'Dave is just a young man who's watched a lot of horror movies.'

'Where is he now?'

'I don't know.'

'But he's still on this plane of reality at least?'

'I hope so. It's his turn to open up the office tomorrow morning.'

There was a knock at the door and Moynahan poked his head around. 'Can I have a word, guv?'

'Is it important? We're just enjoying a new episode of The X-Files.' But Sam could tell from Moynahan's expression that it was.

'Excuse me,' he said to Anne and left the room with Moynahan. Anne and Kelvin sat quietly for a moment until Anne waved a hand at the walls. 'I like what you've done with the place,' she said with a polite smile. Kelvin folded his arms. The universal language of the unimpressed.

On the other side of the door, Sam bellowed a swear word. Followed by several others. In fact, the imagination he displayed in his combination of expletives impressed Anne.

After a while, the invective from the corridor died down and Sam stepped back into the room. A look of worry and confusion had replaced the wry smile he'd been wearing when he left the room.

'Something the matter, guv?' Kelvin asked, concern in his voice.

'It looks like a tube train has made an unscheduled stop at another plane of reality.'

DEATH SENT DAVE home. What he needed to discuss would be between him and his new sister. He was hungry, so they went into the nearest pub that advertised food. Death had never experienced hunger before. It gnawed at his stomach, which seemed to contract minute-to-minute until he thought it would compress itself into a singularity and consume him whole.

They ordered at the bar.

'Starters?' asked the barmaid.

'Yes, please,' replied Death.

'Which one?'

'All of them.' Death turned to his companion. 'Would you like anything?'

She shook her head.

'And for your main?' Death ran a finger down the menu.

'Steak. Medium rare, please.'

'And to drink?'

'I suppose you've never drunk before, have you?' Death asked Azrael.

'No.'

'We'd better ease you in gently, then.' Death turned to the barmaid. 'Two whiskies.'

When they'd been served, they took their drinks to a vacant table. Azrael sipped at the dark brown liquid then, with one action, threw the rest of the drink down her throat. She waved the glass at the barmaid. 'Another!'

'Not bad for someone less than twenty-four hours old.'

Azrael wiped her lips on her sleeve. 'How old are you?'

Death shrugged. 'I'm not sure. Slightly younger than the very first human.'

'What happened to you? Where did you get this bag of meat you're trapped in?'

More shrugging. 'Let it be a lesson on the dangers of alcohol.'

Azrael looked around the busy bar. 'Nobody seems to heed that lesson.'

'For most of these people, life is a series of minor disappointments interspersed with suppressing the feelings produced by those disappointments with booze.'

'That doesn't seem like a brilliant use of a life.'

'Welcome to humanity. It's a lovely place to visit, but I wouldn't want to live here.'

'But you do live here now. What are you going to do?'

'Now you're here, it doesn't matter what I do. I have the whole of my life, however finite that is, stretching before me. This is a new beginning, and I'll finally have an ending.'

'You almost sound like you mean it.' Azrael froze. 'Listen! Can you feel that?'

'Feel what?'

'Worlds are colliding,' Azrael said in hushed tones. 'No, that's not right. Not colliding. Melting. Worlds are melting together.'

'That'll be the whisky,' Death said, finishing the last drops in his glass.

'No, you old fool. There's a crack in the universe and realities are bleeding together. It's close by.'

'How close?'

'In this city.'

'Well, we'll have a look at it when we've finished dinner.'

'We should go now, before it disappears.' The barmaid placed two fresh glasses of whisky in front of them. Azrael looked at them thirstily. 'Well, it'd be rude to leave a drink.'

Just then, the door to the bar swung open and somebody vaguely familiar to Death walked in. Recognition came crashing down, falling on him like a piano in a cartoon. It was Four Finger Freddie from the night before. He clocked Death and walked over.

'Well, if it isn't the weirdo from last night,' he said, leaning menacingly over the table. He turned to Azrael. 'You don't wanna be hangin' around with this one, darlin'. He gets his kicks being slapped around by fellas.'

'You don't be starting any trouble, Freddie,' the barmaid yelled while she poured a pint.

'Is this man a friend of yours?' Azrael asked Death.

'I don't think so,' he replied.

'Come on, now, that's not a pleasant thing to say. You've got me all upset.' Freddie rolled his shirtsleeves up. 'I was gonna let bygones be bygones but, since you said that, why don't we finish what we started last night? Then me and the bird here can get to know each other.'

'Oh, I don't think you'd want to get to know me,' Azrael said with a smile you could slice diamonds with. Freddie moved closer. He would have been invading Azrael's body space if she had what she would term a body.

'Oh, I think I definitely want to get to know you. What's your name?' Azrael looked up and beckoned him closer with a finger.

'Come here and I'll tell you.'

Freddie leaned closer until his ear was almost touching her lips. She whispered something to him and his ruddy face turned white in an instant. A dark stain grew on his jeans, starting at the groin and then running down his leg. The entire bar watched him turn and run, out of the door and down the road.

At that moment, a waitress arrived with a loaded tray.

'Ooh! Prawn cocktail!' Death exclaimed, clapping his hands together.

ANNE, SAM AND Kelvin blued and two-ed it back to Canary Wharf, Kelvin behind the wheel, and parked the car on a street near to the pedestrianised zone. Sam was out first, with Anne and Kelvin following close behind, and they walked to the tube station entrance where an angry crowd wanting to get home had formed. Sam nodded to the officer guarding the top of the escalator, and descended to a deserted concourse.

Through the ticket gates and down another set of escalators, they marched over to the westbound platform. There, a British Transport Police colleague threw blue overalls at them and directed them into the dark mouth of the tunnel.

'Everyone's down there, sir. It's a couple of minutes' walk.'

Sam, wobbling on one leg, pulled the overalls over his suit. He walked to the edge of the platform where the glass safety barrier had been jimmied open and, even though he knew the power had been turned off and all trains pulled out of service, he still had to fight every instinct of self-preservation to jump down onto the tracks. He turned and helped Kelvin and Anne down, and the BTP officer passed them two heavy, rubberised torches.

'Ready?' he asked Anne.

'Let's go.' She radiated an eagerness Sam didn't share.

Entering the tunnel was an eerie feeling, and Sam could hear Kelvin murmuring nervously over his shoulder. The platform behind them retreated into a thin crescent of light as they followed the bend until it slipped away and the only illumination came from the twin circles of torchlight bobbing and weaving ahead of them.

The walk took as long as the officer told them it would and they soon reached a group of confused police officers in matching ill-fitting overalls, all staring blankly at a deserted London Underground train. They had set portable lighting rigs up, twisting shadows into unfamiliar shapes, and the train looked like a dormant mother ship on the set of a science fiction movie.

While the officer in charge of the scene briefed Kelvin, Sam shone his torch along the length of the metal tube. He counted the carriages. He counted them again. Six. And a perfectly spaced gap in the middle where a seventh should've been, as if some giant predator had gouged it out.

'What do you think?' he asked Anne at his side, their shoulders touching. She turned and whispered in his ear.

'Wormholes.'

Sam gave her a doubtful look and shouted to Kelvin over her shoulder. 'How many people were on board?'

'We're still waiting on the CCTV footage, sir.'

'Have we notified Forensics?' A question asked when you didn't know what to do next. Shut the nerds away with their toys and gadgets while you went and got a cup of tea and tried to come up with a plan.

'On their way. What do you think? Do we need to get Counter-Terrorism involved?' Kelvin asked. Sam sighed.

'Buggered if I know.'

'Wormholes,' Anne repeated in a sing-song voice. She could feel incredible power down here, that was undeniable. It was making her lightheaded and giddy.

Sam climbed a stepladder set up next to the front carriage and shone his torch through the window. The aisle was littered with abandoned bags and free newspapers.

'Where are the passengers from the other carriages?' he asked.

'We've evacuated them upstairs, guv. Uniform are interviewing them.'

'And what did they say?' asked Anne.

Kelvin told them the same story jotted down in a dozen notebooks. There'd been a flash of intense light and suddenly there was a big black hole where the fourth carriage used to be. Sam climbed back down to the filth and muck of the tracks and stroked his moustache; something he did when deep in thought. How could someone steal a moving train carriage in a tunnel? Why would someone want to?

'What have we told the press?'

'Gas leak requiring evacuation of the station and holding of the trains in the tunnel.'

'Forensics are here, guv,' someone called from behind him.

'Excellent,' Graves said to Kelvin. 'Let's get a cuppa.'

FORENSICS WAS TURNING into a four-cuppa job, so Sam suggested he and Anne get something to eat while Kelvin waited for the results. They found a chain fast-food restaurant in a nearby shopping arcade and ordered something quick and simple.

As they sat on plastic chairs, making polite conversation and eating disappointing burgers, Sam learned that Anne was smart and funny. She was also as mad as a sack full of badgers, of course, but he could almost forget that.

'How long have you been in the police?' Anne asked, eyeing a suspicious slice of gherkin.

'I joined straight out of university. It's the family business,' he replied, repeating the well-worn Graves joke.

'So that inspired you?'

'Well, that and Inspector Gadget. Though disappointingly I haven't had much use for the extendable arms in my career so far.'

'What did you study at university?'

'History.'

'What's your specialism?'

'The social history of the nineteenth century. It's when my family first became involved in law enforcement. In fact, I'm digitising one of my ancestor's diaries. Fascinating stuff. That's where I read about the Gentlemen of Dubious Activities.'

Sam smiled when he saw Anne's expression. 'Don't look so surprised. Coppers aren't meatheads. Well, maybe Moynahan is. We're fully rounded individuals with lives, dreams, and a surprisingly comprehensive collection of French New Wave cinema.'

'I love the French New Wave! It's so hard to find people who enjoy European cinema these days. I recently went on a date with a man who thought Jean-Luc Godard was the guy who captained the Enterprise.'

'I just think everyone would look better if the world was in black and white and we all spoke French. So, you're not seeing anyone at the moment?'

Anne shook her head. 'My line of work makes it difficult to hold down a steady relationship, y'know?'

'Yeah. How long have you been doing whatever it is you do?'

'Just over a decade now,' Anne replied when she'd completed the mental arithmetic. Then, to herself, 'Wow, has it been that long?'

'Do you need any qualifications?'

'No, but you have to have a knack for it. It's something I fell into. I wasn't in a good place in my life and my boss came along and helped me at the right time.'

'He sounds like an OK guy.'

'He has his moments.'

'Whereabouts do you live?'

'I've got a little place I bought a few years ago, but I'm sure you know all about that, Inspector.'

Sam smiled. 'This isn't another interview. It's just two people making small talk and enjoying a burger.'

Anne looked at the flaccid burger drooping in her hands. 'The word "enjoying" is doing a lot of heavy lifting in that sentence.'

'What did you order?'

'It's called the Large Yummy and I can think of at least two things wrong with that name.'

With everything going on in his world, Sam couldn't remember the last time he'd had an ordinary conversation like this. It felt good: an island of normality in a sea of oddness.

'Have you always lived in London, then?' he asked. Anne wasn't used to being asked so many questions by a man her own age. They usually only wanted to talk about themselves; what car they drove, their jobs, their bitch of an ex-wife. True, quizzing people came naturally to someone in Sam's position, but he was taking an interest and that made her feel good.

'Yes, the family's always lived in the city, going back generations. Some had to circle back, though.'

'What do you mean?'

'My grandfather on my mum's side was from the States. He met my nan during the war, they married and he ended up staying here. He died before I was born, but the story is his grandmother - my great-great-grandmother; her name was Elizabeth or something - moved from London to America when she was a child. My mum told me grandad had said that arriving in London for the first time was like coming home. The city was in his blood. What about the Graveses?'

'Nothing so interesting. We've always been here. I had a cousin who completed a Gold Run on Blockbusters, though.'

'Impressive.'

'Not really. He only got a Sony Walkman out of it.'

The conversation staggered to a halt and the two ate in silence for a moment. Sam thought there'd been enough informal chit-chat to allow him to return to the questions he wanted to ask. 'What happened in the tower?'

'Exactly what I told you.'

'But what you told me is batshit crazy.'

'You said it yourself. Once you eliminate the impossible, whatever remains, no matter how batshit, must be the truth.'

'But it *is* impossible.'

'It's not. More than one reality exists. It's standard quantum physics. You've seen it happen three times now, once to yourself. Are you really going to deny the evidence of your own eyes? And it's getting more serious. Innocent members of the public are involved now and you have a duty to do something about it.'

Sam chewed on a mouthful of fries, mulling Anne's speech over. 'Okay, let's say this is the truth. I have some questions. Where are those passengers? Are they wherever Conrad West is? Is this where all my socks go? Is it going to get worse and worse until it swallows everything up? If so, what do we do about it?'

Sam's mobile phone started vibrating on the table. It was Kelvin. 'Hold that thought,' Sam said. He picked the phone up and answered the call, 'Yes?'

He nodded as Kelvin updated him. 'We'll be right there.' He hung up the call and looked back at Anne.

'They've downloaded the CCTV footage from the other carriages. And we need to bring Kelvin a Large Yummy with bacon.'

'IT'S A POSTBOX,' Melanie said, confused.

'Not just any postbox. Danger Mouse lives beneath it,' Dave explained, pointing to a kerb stone.

'Who's Danger Mouse?'

'Sometimes I think you and I are very different people. Take a photo of me.'

Dave was back on Baker Street and had dragged Melanie along. They had swept away all signs of the accident earlier on that day, the traffic flowing again as if nothing had happened. Dave wrapped his arm around the red postbox as if it were a celebrity agreeing to a picture with a fan. Melanie folded her arms.

'Is this why you brought me here? You said you'd take me to dinner.'

'I will once we get this photo done,' Dave replied, sticking one thumb up, ready for the shot. Melanie didn't move. 'What's up? You said you wanted to see more sights in London, that all this culture surrounded us, but it was passing us by.'

'I meant the British Museum, or the National Portrait Gallery.'

Dave's head dropped. 'Yeah, you're right. I'm sorry, Death and I were supposed to come here today, but he's gone off with his new girlfriend.'

Melanie softened. 'Are you jealous?'

Dave shook his head. 'No. Maybe I'm just finding it hard to process what's happened. It's not every day you wind up with Death sleeping on your couch.'

'But he's not sleeping on your couch, is he? He's not Death, he's Steve. If you were to drop dead on this street, who'd come along?'

'Fair point.'

'Now, let's get this photo done and you can take me to that Korean restaurant I like as payment.'

Dave assumed his previous position and Melanie took a picture on her phone. When Dave had approved it, they walked down the street towards the tube station, Melanie wrapping her arms around Dave's.

'So, what happens job-wise?' she asked.

'What do you mean?'

'Is this new Death your boss now?'

'I hadn't thought about it, to be honest,' Dave said with a shrug.

'You didn't think to ask while they were both there?'

'They said, "take the rest of the day off" and I kinda stopped listening after that.'

'What does Anne think?'

'I've not talked to her. She went off this morning with a policeman and hasn't been back since.'

'What's that about?'

'They're still looking into UberSystems Tower disappearing, but she says it's nothing to worry about. She left me a message. She also said to stay away from the Jubilee line, but that's just common sense.'

'Did you call her back?'

'Yeah, but it goes through to her voicemail.'

'You're useless, you know that, don't you?'

'Oh, fully aware.'

SAM AND ANNE walked back over to the tube station, Sam carrying a paper bag containing Kelvin's dinner. They ducked under the blue and white tape stretched across the station entrance, and Anne nodded to the officer on duty. She was getting the hang of this policing lark.

They found Kelvin in the station office just off the main concourse. Black and white monitors filled one wall, showing the station from different angles and locations, all of them deserted.

Between mouthfuls of meat, Kelvin briefed them with what he had found out. The train - 1996 stock comprising seven carriages - arrived at Canary Wharf Underground Station at 16:13. Platform CCTV showed four passengers alight from the central carriage and three boarded. When the train continued its journey at 16:14, it was carrying seventy-eight passengers and one driver. Fourteen were in the missing carriage.

When in the tunnel, the train was held at a stop signal and witnesses reported a blinding flash of blue-tinted light at 16:15. The fourth carriage was no longer visible between the third and fifth. Forensic tests had found no explosive residue and, anyway, the SCD 4 unit had confirmed that no incendiary device could vaporise that amount of metal. Initial inspection showed no inconsistencies or fractures in the tunnel walls or floor. The track beneath had passed all recent inspections.

The carriage, and its passengers, had disappeared.

'Have we got any intelligence on the passengers?' Sam asked when Kelvin had finished his rundown.

'Well, we ran the footage through the experimental facial recognition software that we definitely don't have,' Kelvin said, looking at Anne out the side of his eye. 'We've identified eight of the fourteen. Two have minors: disturbing the peace and possession. One's flagged as working for the Home Office. That might be worth following up. But, as far as I can see, it's just a random cross-section of the ordinary people of Old London Town.'

'I need to get my boss to come down and look at this,' Anne said, sliding her phone out of her pocket. 'Then I want to go back down there after I've spoken to him.'

'Fair enough.' Sam looked at his watch. 'I'll get my neighbour to feed my cat again.'

'You've got a cat? What breed?'

Sam shrugged. 'An orange one? He's called Serpico.'

Anne smiled. 'Mine's Schrodinger. He's lovely.'

'Mine's a git. Does yours keep trying to sit on your lap when you're working? I do not understand how Bond villains get anything done.'

Kelvin sighed as he tidied up the debris of his dinner. 'I think that's what henchmen are for, guv.'

Sam ignored Kelvin's comment. 'Right, everyone do what they need to do and I want you all back here in five minutes,' he announced to the room, before wandering off to phone his neighbour.

DEATH'S HEAD WAS heavy. Gravity tried to pull it downwards, and he felt that, if he let it, he'd go headfirst through the table, then the earth's crust and mantle, before plunging into the core. With all his strength, he straightened up. Across a sea of glasses and bottles, Azrael still sat opposite.

'Maybe it's time we left,' she said, a look of concern crossing her face.

'But I've still so much to teach you,' Death slurred.

'We can pick up tomorrow where we left off.'

'No, I need to tell you some things. Things you must know.' Death tapped the table with his finger. 'You should write this down.'

'I'm sure I'll remember it.'

'Okay. Point number one: nobody ever said they wish they spent more time in the office. Apart from this one guy, but his kids were just awful.

Two: people are still angry about the ending of something called "Game of Thrones", even though it ended ages ago, and some will even take it beyond the grave. Get yourself the box set or you will spend a lot of time listening to a lot of made-up words that mean nothing to you.

Three: listen to them, rather than talk. For some, this will be the first time they've been heard. They will learn life is not to be won or lost, but to be savoured. This will anger some and comfort others.

Four: we have no official stance on whether there is a God. I've seen plenty of stuff to suggest his existence, but people do a hell of a lot to make me think otherwise.

Five: yes, Elvis is dead, but it will surprise people to find out it happened in 1992 fighting vampires in Denmark. You'll get asked this question a lot, even more than the one about God.

These are the people who built the Sistine Chapel, sent probes beyond the limits of the solar system, and made Die Hard. But they're also the people who made 'We Built This City' by Starship a number one smash hit.'

Something caught in Death's throat, his eyes filling with water. He didn't know what this was, but he didn't like it.

'They're an angry, talented, useless, wonderful, feckless, beautiful, fickle, baffling species, but… Just be careful with them.'

A tear ran down his cheek. He wiped it away with a sleeve.

'Come on,' Azrael said with a comforting smile. 'Let's go home.'

More tears followed. Was this sadness? How did humans cope with this? Experiencing it just this once was bad enough. Imagine coping with it over the course of a lifetime. 'I can't. I don't have a home to go to.'

THE DEFENCE MINISTER had taken charge of the situation in the control room, side-lining Carroll, who was sulking in the corner.

'What eyes have we got out there?' the minister asked anybody who might be listening.

'We have authority to access any public CCTV systems,' Rose replied.

'Does that include TFL's cameras?'

'I'm already on it,' Rose said, spinning round in her chair to type on the keyboard at her workstation. Carroll had never seen her that motivated by anything he'd asked her to do. In fact, the entire room was alive with chatter and activity. Theories were being discussed, solutions proposed. One small group of engineers had already begun work on a computer model of the tunnels below them. He just had to resign himself to the fact that he wasn't a natural leader. He was not one to inspire men to follow him into battle. To be honest, he'd be lucky if he inspired anybody to pop down to the shops to get him a pint of milk.

'I've got them, ma'am,' Rose said proudly.

'Excellent. Put it on the screen.'

The large screen hanging from a wall perpendicular to the observation window flickered into life. Carroll recognised the grainy footage as the platform at Canary Wharf where he'd arrived that morning. It was deserted except for a policeman who stood at the platform's edge, picking his nose.

'Where's the train?' Arden asked, frustrated.

'The event occurred inside the tunnel, ma'am,' Rose explained. 'This is the closest we can get.'

The minister put her hands on her hips. 'Well, this isn't any good. Why don't they have any in the tunnels?'

'Because it's dark and there's usually nobody there,' Carroll chimed in. 'The government would complain if Transport for London had spent money installing cameras that couldn't film anything.'

Though he felt bad, he smiled to himself. Rose had let the minister down so quickly. He adopted a more serious expression when he saw Mills, the military liaison, marching over to him. He grabbed a pile of papers from a nearby desk and shuffled them.

'What is it, Mills? I'm very busy,' he said when the soldier came to attention in front of him.

'Yes, sir. I can see that. I'm very sorry,' Mills humoured him. 'Those individuals from earlier on today? We've traced their identities.'

Carroll glanced over to the minister. Something else was preoccupying her now. 'Keep your voice down, Captain. What have you got?'

Mills produced a folder from under his arm and presented it to Carroll. Inside were two photographs blown up from the footage they'd filmed. 'He is Detective Chief Inspector Samuel Graves of the Metropolitan Police Force. Her name is Anne Mitchell, and she's a civilian.'

'Do you know where they are now?'

'No, but we've traced their home addresses. I can have units to their properties in the next five minutes if you give the word.'

'What are you two talking about?' the minister shouted across the room. Carroll closed the folder.

'Nothing, Your Right Honourableness.'

'Then you won't mind sharing it with the entire class?'

'Really, it's a trivial matter.'

'What's in the folder, Dr Carroll?'

Carroll sighed, crossed the room and handed the green folder to the minister. She flicked the cover open and stared at the photographs. 'Who are these people?'

'Earlier on today there was a similar event on a smaller scale and it involved them.'

'We recorded footage, if you'd like to see it?' Rose said.

'Yes, I would,' replied the minister.

Rose already had the clip cued up and projected it onto the big screen. The film on a loop, the minister watched Sam and Anne disappear again and again.

'We'd calculated the exit point to be at Canary Wharf tube station. Funnily enough,' Carroll laughed nervously, 'by the time we'd got there, they'd gone.'

The minister closed the folder, her mind made up. 'Right, here's what I want done.'

'Dr Carroll,' Rose said. He ignored her.

'I want these two picked up as soon as possible.'

'I have units standing by,' Mills told her.

'Dr Carroll,' Rose repeated.

'How are the Metropolitan Police going to react when you pick up one of their officers? Won't that cause problems with the Home Office?' asked Carroll.

'The Home Office will do whatever I bloody tell them,' said the minister. 'This is a matter of national security.'

'DR CARROLL!'

'Yes, what is it, Rose?'

'Nothing much, sir. I was just seeing whether you want to pick up our two people of interest who've just wandered into the tunnel?'

'You what?'

'Well, you've missed them now but I can back the recording up.' Rose switched the image on the big screen to the live stream of the tube line platform. Reversing the video, two figures walked backwards out of the tunnel and climbed back up onto the platform. When she got a good enough shot, Rose pressed pause. It was undeniable. Those were the faces of Graves and Mitchell.

'Scramble your men, Captain,' Arden ordered. 'I want them rounded up and taken for interrogation.'

'I think interrogation is over the top,' said Carroll. 'I was just going to get them a cup of coffee and have a chat.'

The minister pointed at the screen. 'We don't know what they're up to. For all we know, this morning was a test run for whatever they carried out to make that train disappear.'

'I think you're being paranoid.'

'My job is to be paranoid,' the minister said. 'That's how we keep people like you safe. You've invented a new weapon, Dr Carroll. One that literally wipes its target off the face of the earth. Who knows what applications they could use it for, or on what scale? If those two know anything, I want them to tell me. Captain Mills?'

Mills stood to attention. This was more like it. Truth be told, he was tiring of being an overpaid admin assistant. 'Yes, ma'am?'

'I want a unit ready to go as soon as I give the word. And Dr Carroll?'

'Yes?'

'Stay out of the way. You're making the place look untidy.'

WHEN DEATH FINALLY remembered Dave's address, Azrael gave him a lift back, instantaneously travelling across London.

'I could do that if I wanted,' Death mumbled, his eyes half-closed, barely able to stand on the doorstep. 'I just don't feel like it.'

Luckily, Dave and Melanie were in and helped carry him into the living room. They lay him on the sofa, removing his shoes. An old Arsenal duvet was found and draped over Death's prone figure. He closed his eyes, attempting to stop the room spinning, and everyone left. Hushed voices in the hallway. They were probably talking about him. *Whatever are we to do with a problem like Death?* Soon the voices stopped and a few minutes later he heard somebody walk up to the sofa. They said nothing, but placed something on the floor and left the room, pulling the door closed behind them.

Once the room had stopped its rotations, Death opened his eyes and peered over the edge of the sofa. A glass of water and a bucket. He'd have to remember which one was where, or there could be a hideous accident in the night. He lay back, his head resting on a flattened cushion, and basked in the world's silence. There was no sound from the flat, nor from the street below. In his former life, Death had never known such quiet. It had been millennia of toil and fuss, with no opportunity to slip into one pocket of stillness that punctuated normal life.

Then: a noise. A rhythmic drumming that came from all around. It grew louder and louder until it filled his head and body. Then he realised what it was. His heart, every beat another chip away at his life-force. How did this constant reminder of mortality not drive them insane? Here was a bomb strapped inside their chest, counting down to its moment of self-destruction. Sometimes it would be with a bang, raging against the oncoming darkness. Other times a sigh, slipping into the ever after with no argument. Was this why they talked so much and filled the time up with pointless pursuits like golf or local politics? To block out the idea of the abyss that lay ahead?

Perhaps he needed to do that too. When in Rome, and all that. There was an entire world out there. He'd existed within it, but never experienced it. He should change that.

AZRAEL FOLLOWED THE feeling through the streets of London, like walking against the flow of a river until you found its source. That source looked like a building site in reverse. A structure once stood there, but now they were wiping away all evidence of its existence like an embarrassing stain.

She passed through the wooden walls and stepped out onto the vast, flat space picked clean by an army of workers. Walking across the clearing, the power grew stronger, reaching up from deep below, until she reached the centre. Energy danced around her feet like lightning bolts, generated by the friction of worlds rubbing together. If someone could harness this power, who knew what destruction they would unleash? She had to admit, part of her wanted to find out.

But there it was. The tug pulling her towards the next soul cast loose. She would need to pack that thought away for a moment.

'No rest for the wicked,' she muttered to herself, and disappeared into the ether.

SAM CONCENTRATED ON the gap between the carriages as if he was willing the missing one to rise out of the ground and complete the chain. Most of the investigators had gone home, or to break the news of missing passengers to their loved ones, leaving only a handful behind in the eerie half-light of the tunnel.

'I'm calling it a night, guv,' the last remaining uniformed officer shouted across the track.

'Yeah, you do that, Horner. Get some rest. Give Sandra my love,' Sam called back.

'I will do. Goodnight, Miss Mitchell,' Horner said with a smile.

Anne mirrored Horner's grin. 'Goodnight, and call me Anne.'

'Yes, Miss Mitchell.'

Horner disappeared into the darkness, leaving Sam and Anne alone.

'They all seem to like you,' Anne said.

'Who? The other officers? Yeah, I think they think I'm alright. There can be some rivalry between the lids and the suits, but I just abide by one simple rule.'

'What's that?'

'Don't be a dick.'

Anne nodded. 'That's definitely simple.'

Sam shrugged. 'It's got me this far in life.'

'I know a few people who'd benefit from obeying that rule more. We should probably call it a day too. Sleep on it and come back tomorrow. I'll bring my boss down. Though I hate to admit it, he's smarter than the both of us and has far more experience with this kind of thing.'

'Yeah, you're probably right,' Sam sighed.

'I must warn you that this investigation will get two-hundred percent more annoying.'

Anne assumed Death could still go out in public. Judging by yesterday's performance, he and Dave had probably spent the day at Alton Towers, or something. She didn't know which one was the worse influence on the other. At least this way she could monitor Death and work on a way to get him back to his old grim self.

A silence had fallen between them, but it was different to the one that had filled the car that morning. Now there was a tension. Anne sensed Sam was straining to ask something.

'Listen, do you fancy a quick drink? It's not that late and we should work out a plan for tomorrow. There's a nice place in your neck of the woods. It has a jukebox. You never seem to get jukeboxes in pubs any more, do you? But it's not too loud.' He realised he was gabbling now, but he dreaded the silence that might follow if he stopped. He hoped she'd interrupt him before he said something stupid. 'I can't stand it when you can't hear what people are saying. It's not a nightclub. I've come to a pub for a beer and a chat, right?'

Anne detected the nerves in his voice. It was sweet, really. This was a man who'd sweated down armed robbers and chased murderers and, here he was, getting anxious about asking her out. He would not stop talking, so she should probably answer him.

'A drink sounds a great idea,' she said with a smile.

'Oh, brilliant. That's just—'

Raised voices barking orders echoed along the length of the tunnel.

'What's that?' Anne asked. Sam strained to hear what was happening on the platform. An argument.

'I should check on them,' he said, picking his torch up. Anne instinctively grabbed his arm.

'Don't go. I've got a bad feeling about this.'

'DCI Graves. Ms Mitchell,' a voice called in the darkness. 'I'm Captain Mills, regional liaison officer for the Ministry of Defence. I'd be very grateful if you'd return to the station platform.'

'What's the military doing here?' Sam hissed.

'I don't know, but the reasons can't be good.'

Sam looked down the tunnel toward Mills's voice, then back at Anne. He was in two minds. 'We should go back and find out what they want. The thing is, though—'

'Yes?'

'I've seen this movie and I really don't want to.'

'Nor me.'

'What's that way?' Sam pointed down the tunnel in the opposite direction to where Mills was.

'Canada Water station.'

'The line's closed between here and there. Fancy a walk?'

Anne nodded. 'Sounds a great idea.'

MILLS WAITED PATIENTLY on the platform. The two police officers left on duty were on their knees, hands behind their heads, guarded by two of the five black-clad soldiers he'd led down there.

'You sure they haven't left?' he asked Horner.

'Yeah,' he answered, nodding his head. 'Nobody but me's gone in or out for half an hour.'

Mills looked over at two of his unit, watching over the escalators.

'Johannson! Garvey!' They snapped to attention. 'Get in there and bring them back.'

'Sir!' They jumped down onto the tracks and disappeared into the darkness.

Mills knew Graves and Mitchell wouldn't come out. He would have been disappointed if they had.

LAS VEGAS. PLAYGROUND of America. But a playground where there's a weird guy by the swings and you lose all your money on the roundabout.

Joey 'The Fish' DiMarco looked down on the city; a collection of gaudy jewels scattered in the Nevada desert. From the penthouse of West's Casino and Hotel, he felt as if he could scoop those jewels up and put them in his pocket. A large proportion of them already were.

DiMarco was a dangerous man in a dangerous city. He was feared and respected in equal measure, but sometimes it didn't hurt to flex a little muscle. That was why two of his goons were sweating down one of Frank Donatelli's captains in a warehouse on the other side of town.

He knew things needed to be done a certain way, but acts like this had made Joey increasingly uneasy over the years to a point where he'd had to start therapy. It had been no help, which is why he'd changed his therapist - from a healthy, living therapist to little chunks of therapist dissolved in a motel-room bath. He'd felt bad afterwards, but had nobody to talk to about it.

There was a knock on the suite's door and one of Joey's men let in Eight Ball Eddie.

'They're ready for you, boss.'

Joey fastened the button of his $5,000 suit jacket across his ample belly. 'Thanks, Eddie.'

They took the private elevator down to the ground floor. After pressing some flesh in the lobby, Eddie led Joey through the kitchen and into a black sedan parked in the alleyway at the back of the hotel. It pulled out onto the Strip, anonymous amongst the traffic, and headed for the industrial district.

Around half an hour later, the car pulled up by a warehouse on the edge of the city where the concrete surrendered to the desert. The mountains carved a black pattern in the clear night sky and, when he stared at them, it felt like there wasn't a single living creature between them and him.

'Are you coming, boss?' Eddie asked, standing at his right hand. Joey turned to him.

'Sure.'

Eddie rapped his knuckles three times on the door. There was a snap of a lock opening and a large, bald head poked out.

'Hi, Miguel,' Eddie said.

'Eddie! Mr DiMarco! Come on in,' Miguel politely replied. He held the door open just enough to let the two men through.

The warehouse was empty, pools of light from the fluorescents suspended from the ceiling on barren concrete. In the centre was a chair and tied to that chair was Harry Spinks. Joey remembered Harry as a handsome man; high cheekbones and curly hair the girls loved to run their fingers through. Not now, though. His face was puffy, bruised a livid purple, and his hair matted with sweat and blood.

'Where's Charlie?' Joey asked.

'He's gone to get something to eat,' Miguel replied. 'You know how slappin' people about makes him hungry.'

Joey crossed the warehouse floor.

'How you doin', Harry?' Harry looked up at him, barely able to see through the swollen skin around his eyes and too tired to reply. 'Because you don't seem to be lookin' too good.'

Joey playfully pinched Harry's cheek and wiped the gunk and blood off his fingers on the arm of Harry's filthy, crumpled suit. 'Miguel here says you ain't been too talkative and, you know me Harry, I like a chat. When I was a kid, my Pa said I could talk the hind legs off a donkey. And here you are, sat there so silent and still that you'd think you were bein' shaved by a blind man. That's just rude, Harry.

So why don't you show us some good manners and talk to us? Frankie's got something planned, we just wanna know what it is. Then we cut you loose and you can go back to your wife and kids.'

Harry smiled with swollen lips and spat at Joey, a thick glob of blood and saliva that landed with accuracy on his crisp, white shirt. Joey hit him with a backhand across the jaw. Eddie was already prepared with a handkerchief to clean his knuckles.

When he'd wiped his hands clean, Joey held one out to Miguel, who pulled an automatic pistol from inside his jacket and placed it in his boss's open palm.

'Maybe you should think about this, Joey,' Eddie said, taking a step back. Joey didn't think, just pointed the gun and pulled the trigger. Harry's body jerked against the tight ropes and went limp. Joey sighed and looked at the dark red stain on his shirt.

'I'm gonna send my dry cleanin' bill to your grievin' fuckin' widow.' Then the remorse kicked in. He shouldn't have done that, but Harry had shown disrespect and sometimes his anger got the better of him. Oh well, nothing a quick journey out into the desert in the trunk of a car wouldn't sort out.

'What's going on here?' Azrael asked the ghost of Harry Spinks. Harry tore his eyes away from his battered corpse and looked her up and down.

'Who the fuck are you?'

'I the fuck am Azrael, the Angel of Death.'

'You don't look like no Death I've ever seen.'

'Well, it's usual to only ever see me once, so I don't know who you were looking at previously, but it wasn't me.' Azrael walked around the chair, looking from Harry's body to the three men stood around it, her gaze finally resting on the gun in Joey's hand. 'So they tied you to a chair and shot you? That doesn't seem very fair. What had you done?'

'That's none of your business.'

'You're not going to tell me?'

'Snitches get stitches.'

'It's a bit late for that now.' Azrael looked back at Joey and the smoking gun. 'Nope, I'm not standing for this. It's out of order.'

She stepped gracefully into the mortal world. 'You with the gun. What do you think you're playing at? You can't go round tying people to chairs and shooting them. It's rude.'

Joey looked at Azrael in disbelief. 'Where the fuck did you come from?'

'Never you mind where I came from. How do you explain all this?' She pointed a finger at the bloody scene.

'Let's not cause a ruckus,' Harry said. 'What's done is done.'

Azrael wheeled round to face Harry. 'Let's not cause a ruckus? These men tied you to a chair and killed you. I can think of few things more ruckus-worthy.'

'They were doin' what they had to do. I'd do the same if I was in their shoes.'

Azrael looked at him with horror. 'You are not pleasant people.'

Joey put on the charm. 'Who you talkin' to, doll-face? We're good people. What you say I take you for a drink and you can tell me what's up?'

'I'll tell you what's up,' Azrael said with cold fury. 'Since I've been born into this world, all I've seen is murder, persecution, lies and duplicity. What you've done here is not right. You must pay for this. The scales must be balanced.'

'How you gonna do that?'

She thought for a moment, then clicked her fingers and the universe skipped a beat. Three dead bodies hit the floor. Later, the coroner wouldn't be able to confirm a cause of death. As far as he could tell they had simply stopped living.

A satisfied smile crossed Azrael's face. 'Yes, that will do.'

ANNE AND SAM ran through the tunnel, stumbling along the tracks, torch beams cutting through the dark and dust, catching brief glimpses of creatures scurrying for a hiding place. Anne wondered if there was a way to join them. They had to put as much distance between themselves and their pursuers as possible. Anne didn't know how long they'd run for, she could only measure the distance by how heavy her legs grew and how much her lungs burned. She didn't stop, though. A few years earlier she'd taken part in a 10K run, but her time had disappointed her. Turns out all you needed is to have someone carrying light armaments chase you.

Then, a tiny pinprick of light appeared in front of them, growing larger with every faltering step. Before Anne knew it they had breached the darkness and made it to Canada Water station. The passengers waiting behind the security screens on the platform looked at them with wide-eyed terror. Anne realised why when she felt the low rumble travel up her tired legs. They were on the live track now, and the Jubilee line train was coming into the station. She and Sam pulled frantically at the safety doors, their muscles straining, helped by the commuters on the other side of the glass.

'Stop, or we will open fire!' a voice shouted from the blackness behind them as Anne glanced to her right and saw the twin headlights of the oncoming train. Shot or squashed? Which way would she want to go? And there she was, hoping her cause of death would be old age or magic ninjas.

Suddenly the doors jerked, then slid apart smoothly. Multiple hands reached down and pulled Anne up onto the platform as the train slowed to a halt, sealing the soldiers in the tunnel. She clambered to her feet, hands on her knees, feeling like she might throw up.

'We've got a few minutes before the train leaves,' Sam said, looking a similar shade of might-puke. He took her hand, and they pushed their way through the crowd gathered around them, ignoring the protests and calls for them to stay where they were. They rested on the escalator, getting their breaths back and collecting their thoughts, when the high-pitched beeps of the train doors warned them they were about to close and it was all going to start again. They walked up the escalator, slowly at first, but picking up speed. Though her vision was blurring, Anne could see the ticket barriers shut at the top. Sam had seen the same thing and was fumbling in his wallet for his Oyster card. This was the one time it would be very important to have it ready before reaching the gate. All Anne's cards were in her purse in her handbag back on the platform at Canary Wharf.

'Can I borrow a card?' she wheezed. Sam nodded and held out his debit card. Anne reached out and plucked it from his fingers. The echoing metallic clang told them that whoever was chasing them had reached the escalators and were closing in.

They slapped the cards on the readers next to the barriers. The barriers whirred open, letting them spill through, and jerked shut behind them. With a few more steps, they were on the street and blending into the throng. Anne handed Sam his card back.

'We didn't touch in. They'll charge you the maximum fare.'

SAM PEERED OVER the wall at the edge of the wharf. From this vantage point across the way from the underground station he could see the officer who'd been on guard had been replaced by a trim man in black combat gear carrying various instruments designed to hurt people. Some were classics, others would do it in new and interesting ways. Sam ducked back down again and flattened himself against the wall next to where Anne crouched.

'They've got someone guarding the entrance,' he said.

'Why are the army here?'

Sam and Anne had taken a taxi back to Canary Wharf, Sam making sure he got a receipt. After being chased through tunnels by armed soldiers, he'd be damned if his expenses claim wouldn't be allowed because of the incorrect paperwork.

'I don't know. I need to phone this in. Let's get back to the car.'

They shuffled along, crouching low, until they ran out of wall. Then, on a count of three, they stood up and looked as nonchalant as they could while speed-walking to the street where they'd parked a few hours earlier.

Once in the car, they sat in silence for a few seconds, both enjoying the security of the steel shell around them. Sam reached for his mobile phone when it rang. He didn't recognise the number.

'DCI Graves,' he said, answering the call.

'Graves, my man, it's Commander Collins here. We spoke yesterday, remember?'

Sam straightened up in his seat. 'Of course, sir.'

'How are you?'

'I've been better, sir.'

'Marvellous. How's it going with that boring Conrad West case?'

'I'm making headway. I think there's a link to our missing train.'

'That train business, too? All this must be a right old yawn-fest for you.'

Sam could see where this was going, but played dumb. 'What are you getting at, sir?'

'I don't think those cases are worthy of a detective of your calibre. You're being removed as head investigator effective immediately and we're standing all resources down.'

Sam punched the steering wheel in frustration. 'And who will take over? We've still got fourteen people missing.'

115

'There's been some interest from the Ministry of Defence. It aligns with some work they've been doing. They'll be taking over from you.'

'The MoD, sir? That's very irregular.'

'Their boffins want to have a crack at it. Dull, dull, science-y stuff. Wouldn't interest you in the slightest, I'm sure.'

'But, sir, I think I can—'

Collins's tone hardened. 'Drop the case, Graves. That's an order that comes from the very top.'

'Are they the same people at the top who wanted me to find Conrad West yesterday?'

'Look Graves, there are many people at the top and they all want different things. My job is to keep the person I last talked to happy.' Collins sounded tired now. 'It's the military's problem.'

Collins hung up. Sam stared at the telephone in disbelief.

'What's going on?' Anne asked.

'The military has taken over our investigation. A fiver says they'll cover all this up.'

'What makes you say that?'

'That's what they do. Human nature. If it's too difficult to understand, or attracts too many awkward questions, then it's easier to just pretend it's not there and that it never happened.'

'Like you and wormholes?'

'Leave them out of this.'

'What about the missing people?'

'They'll abandon them with some convenient explanation.'

Anne grabbed Sam by the arm. 'We can't let that happen.'

'We just spent the last couple of hours running away from the people sent to deal with it.'

'So what do you suggest we do, then?'

Sam started the car's engine. 'I say we get drunk because I'm fresh out of ideas.'

He pulled out into the traffic, taking the road that looped around the underground station then the road that followed the river. They drove in silence, both tired but happy to be putting distance between themselves and the station.

Anne watched the plasma glow of the city twist and warp in the window. There was something about being driven at night. The empty roads, the closed shops and offices, like theirs was a secret journey known only to them. She'd felt it since she was a child, snug in the back seat of her parents' car, cocooned from the outside world. Sleepy, she looked over at Sam and he looked back, a supportive smile on his lips. She was safe again.

Soon, though, Anne could see there was something going on behind them. Sam's eyes kept darting from the road in front to the rear-view mirror.

'I think we're being followed,' he said. Anne turned in her seat. 'No, don't do that. Keep looking straight ahead.'

'What do we do?'

Sam thought for a moment then, flicking the indicator stalk, turned the car left down a narrow one-way street. The suspicious car did the same. At the bottom of the alley, Sam turned left again onto the main road running parallel to the one they'd been driving on. As did the car behind them. They drove for a little while, heading in the opposite direction they'd been travelling, when Sam turned left into another side road at the last minute. They drove to the end and turned left back onto the road they'd started on, completing the circle. He checked the rear-view mirror again.

The car was still there.

'Yeah, we're definitely being followed.'

'Clever. Where did you learn that? Advanced police training?'

'Nah, Bruce Willis movie.'

Something occurred to Anne then. 'But won't they figure out we know they're following us? Nobody makes three left turns like that.'

'Oh. I hadn't thought of—'

A car similar to the one following them pulled out sharply from a side street. Sam slammed on the brakes, skidding to a halt inches from the driver's door. Before he could register what was going on, three men dressed in black pointing machine guns at him were already out of the car and ordering him to turn the engine off.

Sam did as he was told as the car following him pulled up alongside. More men. More guns. This wasn't SCO19, the Met's firearms unit. These were military friends of the soldiers at the tube station. He instinctively put his hands in the air to show he was no threat.

'Step out of the vehicle,' someone yelled. Sam looked over at a shocked Anne.

'Just do what they say,' he said.

Sam reached for the seatbelt buckle, released it, and did the same to Anne's. With his other hand, he squeezed the door handle and pushed the car door open. Raising his hands again, he stepped out onto the tarmac, six guns trained on him. From the corner of his eye, it relieved him to see Anne imitate his actions. The gunmen moved forward, three on one side of the car, three on the other; military formation.

'Turn round and place your hands on the roof.' Sam did as he was told and immediately one gunman was patting him down. The same thing was happening to Anne on the other side of the car. Their mobile phones were pulled from their pockets, thrown to the ground and stamped on.

'Hey!' Sam shouted. 'I'm going to be very annoyed if I have to start Candy Crush all over again.'

'Well, let this be a lesson on making regular backups,' the gunman said.

When the gunmen were happy that they weren't carrying anything dangerous, their arms were unceremoniously pulled behind their backs and they felt nylon cable ties slip over their wrists and tighten.

Before the cotton hoods were pulled over their heads, Sam made eye contact with Anne.

'It'll be okay.'

The car pulled off as soon as Sam had been bundled in, speeding until he guessed the road they were travelling on had merged with a dual carriageway, or the motorway. He was alone in the back seat; they would've taken Anne in the other car. They were driving out of the centre of London. He'd found enough bodies buried in shallow graves in the woodlands surrounding the city to know that this should worry him.

'This is the worst Uber I've ever been in. Your rating will take a hammering when I get out.' Taking the piss had always helped calm Sam's nerves over the years. If he was going down, he wasn't going down without annoying them.

'If you don't shut up—'

'You'll what? Turn this car round and we won't go to the beach? Jeez, dad, I was only mucking about.' Sam sat back in the car seat and let himself be taken wherever they might be heading.

It relieved him when the car left the main road while still within the city limits. Each turn they took was evidence they were in a narrow rat-run of streets and alleyways. After descending a ramp, the car turned in a wide circle and came to a stop.

The driver killed the engine and Sam braced himself for whatever was to happen next. Both front doors opened and shut. Hands pulled the back doors open, grabbed Sam by the arm and yanked him out of the car onto his feet.

Marched away from the vehicle, Sam guessed they had taken him to an underground car park; there was a chill in the air and the synchronised footsteps of the soldiers either side of him echoed off the concrete. They walked him into a small room and Sam heard doors slide closed behind him. His stomach lurched as he dropped downwards; a lift. Several floors down, a set of doors opened and they frogmarched him along a corridor.

The journey ended with another small room. Without warning, a guard ripped the hood from Sam's head and the world flooded his senses. Before he could regain his composure, a blade slid between his wrists behind his back and sliced through the ties that were cutting into his skin.

He rubbed the raw skin around his wrists and, as his vision focused, he could see he was in a holding cell. It was far too bright and new to be a police custody suite, so white and clean. Only the military had this kind of money thrown at it. Sam turned to see that his chaperones had retreated outside the cell, weapons still trained on him as if he was the most dangerous terrorist they'd ever come across.

'Thanks very much, guys. If I could see the gluten-free menu for dinner, please, and get an alarm call at seven tomorrow?'

Neither guard reacted, other than to slam the cell door shut.

WEDNESDAY

DAVE PLACED AN UberSystems International branded mug on the floor in front of the couch Death snored on.

'Time to get up now. I've made you a coffee,' he said, gently shaking him by the shoulder. Death opened one eye.

'Is it strong enough to drag me out of any pub I might go in?' he croaked.

'I've put so many granules in it's like gravy.'

It was a struggle, but Death pulled himself to an upright position. Dave handed him the mug and he took small sips.

'What did you get up to last night?' Dave asked.

'I took Azrael to the pub to teach her some things about humanity. It all gets fuzzy after that. I remember throwing up. Food is not as pleasant coming back up as it is going down.'

'You have to slow down. You've got a liver now, remember? There's only so much punishment they can take.'

Death nodded his head, then bitterly regretted it. 'I understand. I was drinking to blot out how I feel, but how you feel is part of life, isn't it? I'm only here for a short time, so where's the logic of deliberately wiping chunks of it from my memory?'

Dave patted him on the back. 'That's a good start.'

'Please don't do that,' Death whimpered.

'C'mon, I've got something for you in the bedroom.'

'I'm very flattered, Dave, but I don't swing that way.' Death paused, considering the statement. 'Actually, I don't think I swing that way. I have a sexuality now, I hadn't thought about that. How do you know whether you like boys or girls? Or both?'

'I think most people just know, but some others take a little more time.'

'Did you just know?'

'Yes. Princess Leia in the gold bikini. She made me have thoughts I felt guilty about but didn't understand why.'

'You're such a cliché.'

Dave nodded in agreement. 'It's not the first time somebody has said that to me.'

He helped Death up off the couch and they walked through to Dave's bedroom. Melanie was still under the duvet, drinking tea and watching a reality show on a laptop balanced on her legs.

'Good morning,' she said with a smile. 'How are you?'

'During the night, somebody replaced my original eyes with ones too big for their sockets.'

Melanie nodded knowingly. 'I've been there.'

'So, why did you bring me in here?'

'It's nothing much. You're about my size, so I've picked some clothes out for you.' Dave gestured to a chair under the window on which he'd laid several pairs of jeans and tee shirts. Death picked up the tee shirt at the top of the pile.

'Who is Frankie and why should I listen to him and relax?'

'Yeah, that's from an 80s night I went to a few years ago. I should ignore that advice. "Frankie Says Panic" would be a more appropriate slogan in this day and age.'

'Thank you, Dave.' Death's too-big eyes filled with water again. Damn these chemical imbalances for making him act like this.

'Hey, don't be that way,' Mel said, putting the laptop to one side.

'Oh, it's nothing,' Death said, wiping his nose on the back of his hand. 'I've got to get used to these emotions. They come with the body, right?'

'I'm afraid so,' Dave said with a supportive smile. 'Is there anything we can do to help?'

'I probably need to get some fresh air, or something. Let's finish what we started yesterday. We might even make it to Baker Street this time.' Dave and Melanie exchanged glances.

'Well, Melanie and I sort of did that last night,' Dave said.

'Oh, that's fair enough.'

Melanie shrugged her shoulders. 'It's not all that.'

'I'm sorry,' Dave said. 'I'll tell you what. Why don't you have a shower while I make you some breakfast? Everything will be better after that.'

'In the legendary Quantum Shower of Doom?' Death asked with a sniff. 'It would be an honour.'

'There's a towel in the bathroom. We'll leave you to it.'

DAVE AND MELANIE walked into the kitchen to find Azrael going through their fridge. Dave coughed politely to attract her attention.

'I know you're new here, but it's good manners to announce your arrival at somebody's house, rather than magically transporting yourself into their kitchen and going through their stuff.'

Azrael's head appeared from around the fridge door. 'I'm sorry. I'm still trying to get used to the many rules of etiquette you people have. Why have you got so many of these long green things?'

'The Peperamis? Yeah, they belong to my housemate. It's best not to ask. Would you like a tea or coffee?'

Azrael closed the fridge and turned to face Dave. 'The brown liquid? No, thank you.'

'Fair enough. This is my girlfriend, Melanie,' he said, gesturing to her as she hovered in the doorway. 'Melanie, this is Azrael.'

'*This* is Azrael?' Melanie asked Dave with a pointed look. He nodded. 'You didn't tell me she was this attractive.'

'I hadn't noticed,' he lied.

'Girlfriend? As in, the one you mate with?' Azrael asked. Dave squirmed.

'Yeah, that's one way of putting it.' Azrael turned to Melanie.

'It's a pleasure to meet you.'

'Likewise.'

Gary walked into the kitchen, cleaning an ear out with one finger, when the sight of Azrael startled him. 'Another new one,' he said with the closest he could get to a seductive smile. 'And what's your name?'

'I am Azrael, the Angel of Death, the whisper on the lips of the damned, the dark companion who walks in the shadows—'

'Oh, you're a goth chick. Never mind.' Gary opened the fridge, took a Peperami from a shelf and walked out.

'Where is the-one-who-calls-himself-Steve? I need to tell him about something,' Azrael said when Gary had returned to his bedroom.

'He's in the shower. He'll be out soon. Which is good, because I was hoping we could have a talk, just the two of us.' Dave looked over at Melanie, who got the message and slipped away into the living room.

'I'm always happy to talk to any sentient creatures, whatever they may be.'

'Nobody's ever described me like that before. Do you want to take a seat?' Dave said, sitting down at the small kitchen table pushed up against one wall. Azrael took the chair opposite.

'What would you like to talk about, David Marwood?'

'Everybody calls me Dave. See, the thing is, I worked for the old Death.'

'He hasn't mentioned that.'

'Really? I thought I would've come up at some point.' Azrael shook her head.

'No. In what capacity did you work for him?'

'There were some moments in history where he wasn't that great at doing his job and this means there are a lot of ghosts. I go around and sort them out.'

'You work for him? And all humans can do this?'

'No, there's only two of us. There's Anne, but you haven't met her yet. In fact, I'm not sure where she is.' Dave shifted in his chair. Turns out it's awkward to discuss jobs and money with your boss, whether they're human or pan-dimensional beings. 'So I was checking, as the afterlife is under new management, whether I still had a job?'

Azrael stared at him, nonplussed. 'I am a master of time and space. Why would I need someone to do my work for me? I have all of eternity to complete my tasks.'

Dave felt his stomach drop. 'So I'm unemployed?'

'I'm sure somebody of your calibre and skill set will find other suitable employment.'

'Being able to talk to the dead is a pretty niche market.'

'Maybe something at the funfair?'

'Is there something else I can do for you? I can be, like, a personal assistant? I could pick up your dry cleaning, or arrange for your scythe to be polished?'

'My clothes are a projection of my self-image and a scythe is a little old-fashioned, don't you think?'

'I just think—'

Death walked into the kitchen, towelling his hair dry. 'You're out of shower gel. I had nothing to eat in there. Oh, hello, Azrael.'

Azrael turned in her seat. 'Good morning. I'm glad you're here. This conversation was getting awkward. I need to talk to you in private about a rather urgent matter.'

'Sure, we'll go out somewhere. I fancy sushi. I know a great little place. Let me just finish getting ready.'

'That's fine. Just one thing. Who's Frankie?'

LORRAINE ARDEN MP sat back in the leather chair behind her enormous desk in the underground bunker that came with the job of Defence Minister. Her research assistant was looking into whether they could buy a cat on expenses. It would sit on her lap during Zoom calls to complete the Bond villain aesthetic.

All those years of constituency surgeries listening to insignificant people complaining about the height of their neighbour's trees and hours sat on meaningless committees were paying off. Here she was working to defend the United Kingdom of Great Britain and Northern Ireland from those who may wish to harm the union. This was genuine power. What next? Home Secretary? What could stop her moving the family into Number Ten in a few years?

Picking up the remote control from her desk, the minister turned up the volume on the news report playing on the large television embedded into the bomb-proof wall of her office. As soon as the army had taken over the investigations, she had allowed the release of the train passengers still being interviewed and they were queueing up to tell the networks what they'd witnessed.

Mills had informed her he had picked Mitchell and Graves up in the night and they were in the cells. The icing on the cake, though, was when the investigators she'd assembled had taken possession of the evidence amassed by Graves's team. The image of Mitchell and two as-yet-unidentified associates leaving UberSystems Tower minutes before its disappearance. They would release it to the press in a few hours and she would have an oven-ready terrorist cell to hang the blame for everything on.

A knock on the door disrupted Arden's train of thought. 'Come in,' she yelled. Dr Carroll poked his head around the door and Arden groaned internally. That was her buzz killed for the moment.

'You wanted to see me, Minister?' Arden nodded and beckoned him in.

'We're going to interview the suspects soon,' Arden said, with one eye still on the television.

'The witnesses, you mean,' corrected Carroll.

'Hmm?' Arden turned her head, giving him her full attention.

'You called them suspects, but surely we don't suspect them of doing anything? We're responsible for all of this mess. They had nothing to do with it other than being in the wrong place at the wrong time.'

Arden turned the television off and sat forward in her chair, her fingers steepled in front of her. 'You've spent your entire adult life in academia and you're new to this business, so I'll spell it out for you. We can't let the existence of the Thingummy be known by our enemies and allies. This will be a game-changer. It'll put Britain back on the map.'

'So, what, you're just going to keep them locked up?'

'The various anti-terrorism laws we've brought in over the last couple of decades give us a whole range of options to play with. If I wanted, I could make sure they never see the sun again. It's national security, Carroll. We can't have every Tom, Dick or Harry wandering around London, popping through wormholes. It's just not proper.'

'What do you need me for if you've already played judge and jury?'

'I still need to brief the prime minister. I need to find out how much they know and how they know it. You can ask the right questions. I want you feeding them to my interrogators.'

'It's an interrogation now? It was just an interview a few seconds ago. I need to know. Are you going to hurt them?'

Arden gave her best politician's smile. 'I think the Secret Service prefer to call it 'incentivised questioning'. It all depends how cooperative they are.' She waved Carroll away. 'Off you pop. We'll call when we need you.'

ONE PERK OF being the Grim Reaper is the ability to communicate with every soul on earth, even those that only spoke a language known by a handful of people. But while Death ordered sushi for both him and Azrael in a little out-of-the-way place he liked in Tokyo, he felt himself grasping for words just out of reach. He was becoming a little more human with every language lost.

They sat among the salarymen, Death gorging himself and Azrael picking at the rice and seaweed. 'How did last night go?' Death asked between mouthfuls of tuna and salmon.

'They're so cruel,' Azrael answered. 'Why do they insist on being awful to each other?'

'What happened?'

'Where do I begin? Take these people in Las Vegas, for example. One of them was tied to a chair, and the others had beaten and shot him. Can you believe that?'

Death nodded. This was a familiar story. 'Mob hit? Yeah, seen a few of those in my time.'

'Everything worked out. Everyone died and returned balance to the universe.'

'How did everyone else die? Ambush? Police raid?'

'I killed them,' Azrael replied with a smile. Death froze, a Salmon Maki roll halfway between the plate and his mouth.

'You what now?'

'I killed them. I did to them what they had done to someone else. It seemed only fair.'

'And how did that go down?'

'They weren't thrilled about it.'

'Shocking.' Death put his chopsticks down on the table. 'Listen, you can't go round doing stuff like that.'

'They were bad men.'

'It's not your place to judge whether someone should live or die.'

'Who does the judging, then?'

Death shrugged and picked up the chopsticks. 'Damned if I know, but we just sort out the admin. Promise me you won't do anything like that ever again.'

Azrael took a small notepad and pen from a jacket pocket. She turned to a new page and wrote 'Don't kill people'. 'This kind of advice is invaluable,' she said, flipping the notepad shut. 'How did you cope with all this on your own when you started?'

'The world wasn't so complicated then. They mostly died from disease, or lack of food, or being trodden on by a mammoth. And, after a while, I wasn't on my own. We were the Four Horsemen of the Apocalypse. War, Conquest, Famine, and Death.

129

Four brothers. It was our destiny to bring about the end of the world.'

'You didn't do a wonderful job. It's all still here.'

Death smiled; partly at Azrael's comment, partly at the memory of his friends. 'We abandoned that during the seventeenth century, as far as I remember. Despite their problems, we grew to like and even love the humans.'

'Where are they now?'

Death's smile collapsed at the edges. 'They're all dead.'

'I thought we were immortal?'

'They weren't like us. They were corporeal, physical, governed by the natural laws of this world. A world they saved many times, but now there's nothing to show they even existed.'

'Nothing at all?'

'I had a flaming sword, the only thing I had to remind me of those times, but I left it somewhere and now I don't even know which world it's in.'

'Maybe I'll have three sisters?' Azrael asked, excited.

'The Four Horsewomen of the Apocalypse?'

'I'm not sure I'd want to ride a horse. It looks uncomfortable. What about a bike?'

'The Four BMXers of the Apocalypse? What if the others showed up? Would you destroy the world?'

Azrael thought the question over. 'If that's what I'm here to do. How would I know?'

'You will,' Death replied, and popped the Maki roll into his mouth.

CARROLL WISHED HE'D stayed in his lab under the storeroom at Oxford University. He would've spent years peacefully fiddling with his equations as he grew ever more eccentric, undergraduates laughing at him behind his back as he tried to bend space-time around the college quadrangle. Sure, none of his work would get beyond the theoretical stage, but the only politics he would have to deal with was arguing with the biology professors over the doughnuts in the faculty lounge.

Yes, he'd had ambition, but nothing out of the ordinary. He didn't want much; maybe a Nobel Prize or two, and then perhaps a move into the private sector to bulk out the pitiful annuity he'd receive from the college.

Now, sat in his office looking over the deserted control room, he wondered what his next step should be. The drive that powered his research all those years had dried up. After the minister had dismissed him from her office, he'd taken a government car back to the Canary Wharf research centre. It was the only place that made sense to him. Physics was in charge here and it governed by laying down cast-iron rules.

Since the train passengers had gone public, news crews had assembled at the front of the station, pushed back by the increased number of soldiers guarding the entrance. The monitor on Carroll's desk showed the crowd growing larger, with members of the public gathering to see what all the fuss was about. As he'd walked from the car to the escalators, he'd recognised a handful of reporters and felt a frisson of excitement at being involved in something that held the attention of the big guns of the broadcasting world.

Then, sat here in his office, the only sound the hum of servers, he remembered the fourteen commuters his government had abandoned. And what about the two people looking for them, who they were going to stab in the back? What could the Mitchell woman tell him? She'd been at UberSystems Tower the moment it transdimensionalised. Yes, it was a proper word. Carroll should know. He invented it.

This was his fault, his responsibility. For too long he'd played with the fabric of space-time without heed of the consequences. If people knew what was going on, if there was no way to deny the facts, the public surely wouldn't stand for it. The MoD would have to find the missing passengers. Mitchell and Graves were another matter, though. They could easily disappear. He'd have to think of a way of ensuring their safety, too.

He opened a desk drawer and a quick rummage produced a novelty memory stick shaped like a penguin. With one eye on the door, he pushed it into the USB socket of his desktop. A quick C and V later, files were moving swiftly from the servers into the penguin.

There was a knock at the door and Mills barged his way in. Didn't anybody in the army wait for anything? With one swift movement, Carroll dropped a stack of papers over the memory stick and flicked the monitor off.

Mills eyed him with suspicion, a hand instinctively moving towards the holster strapped to his hip. 'I thought I heard somebody in here. What are you doing, Doctor? What are you looking at?'

Carroll had never been questioned by somebody carrying a weapon before. His stomach turned to water. 'Just some pornography.'

Mills's hand moved away from the revolver. 'Fair enough, sir. I understand it's been a bit stressful for you. I'll... ahem… leave you alone.'

Mills closed the door behind him and Carroll breathed a sigh of relief. A few minutes later, he strolled out of the control room, the memory stick in his pocket containing hundreds of classified Ministry of Defence documents and several episodes of Buffy the Vampire Slayer that Rose had left on the network.

CARROLL RETURNED TO M.O.D.U.L.E. A fictional accountancy firm occupied the offices built over the top of the base as a cover - an accurate re-creation down to the half-dead pot plants and half-asleep security guard in the foyer. Carroll swiped himself through the security barriers, nodding to the guard behind the reception desk. The previous Defence Minister had wanted the entrance to be via a secret lift in a phone box, until the architect advised him it would take the staff over two hours to get to their desks every morning.

As Carroll stepped into the lift, a message landed in the encrypted government communications app on his phone. The prisoners were moving from the detention block four storeys below him soon, and he should make his way to the interrogation rooms on the floor above the cells. A plan had formed on his journey back from Canary Wharf. He would be the first to admit it wasn't a brilliant plan, but he was new to the world of treason. The lift doors closed, and Dr Carroll descended towards M.O.D.U.L.E and his destiny.

CARROLL STEPPED OUT of the lift into a long, empty corridor. The floor was concrete, buffed up to a shine, with doors secured by keypads built into the plain white walls at regular intervals. He headed towards the cells and was glad to see Mitchell and Graves, chaperoned by one of Mills's drones, walking towards him. Carroll recognised the soldier as a private named Garvey; well-known for being a buffoon. This plan might just work.

'There you are, Garvey,' Carroll said in his most serious voice. 'Captain Mills has been looking for you.'

Garvey came to a halt. Anne and Sam, their hands tied behind their backs again, bumped into the back of him. 'But I'm taking the prisoners up to the interview rooms,' said Garvey.

'He did seem rather keen to talk to you. I wouldn't want to keep him waiting with the mood he's in.'

'Is it about what happened in the tunnel?' Garvey asked, his words coloured with worry.

'Is that something that he'd be annoyed about?' Carroll asked, testing the water.

Garvey nodded. 'Yes.'

'Then that's probably what it's about.'

Garvey looked from Carroll to the prisoners and back again, unsure of what to do.

'I'll tell you what,' Carroll said. 'I'm going up to the interview rooms myself. Why don't I take these two with me?'

'But my orders are to—'

Carroll patted Garvey on the shoulder. 'We're over fifty feet below the surface, surrounded by a shell built to withstand a nuclear blast. I'm sure I can get two people to the floor above.'

Carroll wondered if he'd missed his calling. He should've gone into acting. Relief crossed Garvey's face. 'Thanks, sir. Where's the captain?'

'By the armoury.'

Garvey ran to the lift doors. When he'd taken one down into the bowels of the subterranean complex, Carroll checked over the shoulders of Anne and Sam. They were alone.

'My name is Dr Raymond Carroll,' he said in a low whisper. 'I'm the team leader of Project Sisko, which is the reason you're here. If you do what I tell you, I can get you out.'

Sam and Anne looked at each other. 'Well, we've had no better offers today,' Sam said with a shrug.

'Follow me,' said Carroll. He led them along the corridor in the direction Garvey had gone, past the lifts and through a door that led to a stairwell. He pulled a Swiss Army knife from his pocket and cut Sam and Anne loose.

'Why are you doing this?' Anne asked, rubbing her wrists. Carroll climbed the stairs, the metallic ring of his footsteps echoing upwards. Anne and Sam followed him.

'I'm responsible for all this,' Carroll said to her. 'My experiment created the wormhole—'

'Told you,' Anne said with a satisfied grin.

'Yeah, okay,' Sam replied, rolling his eyes.

'—The wormhole through which you travelled and caused the train to leave this reality. You and your friends are going to be scapegoats for all of this. UberSystems Tower, the train, everything.'

'They can't do that,' Anne said.

'Can't they?' Sam replied. 'Look where we are. They could let us rot down here and nobody would ever find us.'

'But there are people still missing.'

'It's in the military's hands now,' Carroll said. 'They'll do nothing about it. I've made a copy of my research,' said Carroll. 'If we can get that out to the public, that will exonerate you and perhaps force the government to search for them.'

Anne looked up at the flight of stairs. 'Surely we can't just walk straight out?' she asked. Carroll checked his watch.

'The fire alarms should go off in about ten seconds.'

'Ah, you've hacked the mainframe to trigger it,' Sam said.

Carroll looked back at Sam, confused. 'No, I paid an intern fifty pounds to set it off.'

135

The shrill cry of the alarm tore the air apart. Within a few seconds, the doors at each landing flew open and bodies filled the stairwell, all heading upwards with the three escapees following.

Workers spilled out into the foyer. Anne, Sam and Carroll lost themselves in the crowd, their heads low until they reached the street. People milled around like confused cattle, herded to assembly points by fire wardens in fluorescent tabards.

'My car's just down the next street,' Carroll hissed. 'Follow me.'

His hands in his pockets, Carroll casually broke away from the main group and ambled along the pavement. Anne and Sam did the same until the three rounded the corner.

Then, they ran.

DEATH STEPPED ONTO Baker Street for the second time in twenty-four hours. Taking care, he crossed at the traffic lights, noticing the thick black trails of melted rubber where he'd been the day before. Some humans were born lucky. Was he one of them?

The coffee Death drank on the way to the station had jump-started his mood and the sun warmed him, burning off his hangover like only a summer's day could. So what if they'd left him on his own? After so many millennia in a customer-facing role, it was good to have a bit of 'me' time. He would spend the day deciding what kind of man Steve Newman was. Today, he was going to be an optimist. To this Steve Newman, the glass was always half-full. Who knew who'd he'd be tomorrow? He could try on different personalities, see which one fit. He had a lifetime to do this before, one day, Azrael came for him. Even if they returned him to immortality, what would be the point? There was someone else doing the job. Forever can be a drag even when you have a purpose. He dreaded to think what it would be like without one.

What would be his raison d'être now? What would add meaning to his life? He had money in the bank. You'd have to be an idiot to live as long as he had without making a few quid. Perhaps he could use it to improve the lives of others? Or blow it all on a vast mansion with a golden statue of Billy Joel in the central courtyard, complete with in-built speakers playing his greatest hits. Or pay the actual Billy Joel to be painted in gold and sit in the central courtyard playing his greatest hits. He could work on the finer details later, he just needed to ask Anne where his debit card was.

Where was Anne, anyway? They hadn't been in touch with each other since yesterday morning. Death took a chunk of brightly coloured plastic from his jeans pocket; an old mobile phone found at the back of a drawer at Dave's flat. He was about to dial Anne's number, the only number he'd ever needed and had committed to memory, when it rang. The single line display read 'Unknown'. He pressed the worn plastic button to answer the call and gingerly held the phone to his ear.

'Hello?'

'Hello,' replied an overly cheery voice from down the line. 'We understand you've recently been involved in an accident that wasn't your fault.'

'One accident? Try bloody millions,' Death said. 'And they all blame you, even though you're just there to sort out the post-mortem administration. You won't believe the things they've called me over the centuries. It's enough to make a sailor blush. Did I make the blimp fall out of the sky, or push them into the volcano?'

'Yeah, alright, there's no need to take the piss mate,' said the caller before he hung up.

'He seemed friendly enough,' Death muttered to himself. He was about to call Anne when the crowds in front of him parted and there it was. Bright red and sure, as if the pillar box had stood there since time immemorial and the world had grown and shaped itself around it.

Death slipped the phone back into his pocket, the call to Anne forgotten, and made his way through the crowd until he was close enough to touch it. He ran his fingers around the pillar box's cap. A shiver ran up his spine. A novel experience for someone who, until forty-eight hours ago, didn't even have one. He needed to take a photograph.

Reaching into his pocket, he remembered that his phone had been manufactured sometime around the last ice age when mobile phones were used to make calls and nothing else. For making digital images, the device was about as useful as a brick.

'What are you doing with my gran's phone?' a voice behind him asked. Death turned around to find Emma stood there. Another shiver.

'Oh, I lost mine. I've borrowed this one from a friend. What are you doing here?'

'It's funny, ever since you mentioned coming here yesterday, I haven't been able to get it out of my mind. I loved that show as a kid. It's my day off, so I thought I'd take advantage of living in London for once.'

This was the first time Death had seen Emma out of her hospital scrubs. She wore a plain white tee shirt and skinny jeans that accentuated the shape of her — Death dropped his gaze, concentrated his attention on the pavement just in front of his feet. What was wrong with him when he was in this woman's presence? Once he was sure his blood had returned to where it should be, he raised his eyes.

Emma nodded towards the pillar box. 'Would you like me to take a picture? If you give me your address, I can email it to you.'

Death smiled sheepishly. 'I don't think I have one of those either.'

'Okay,' Emma said, folding her arms. 'I'll take a picture of you, then you can buy me a drink while I set one up for you.'

LORRAINE ARDEN DRUMMED her fingers on the desktop and counted to ten. When she'd finished, she asked, 'How did they escape the Mensa members in your ranks?'

Mills dropped the severed wrist ties on her desk. 'I don't know yet. We found these in a stairwell on the detention level. I've got people reviewing the security camera footage. We assume they escaped during the fire alarm.'

The minister thought about the Peter Principle; how workers are promoted to their level of incompetence, and what a fluke it was that every single person who reported to her had reached theirs.

'Where's that other member of the Brain Trust that works for me? Dr Carroll?' she asked.

'I have my men looking for him. Nobody's seen him since Mitchell and Graves escaped.'

Arden put two and two together, and the answer made her scream internally. 'Find them. Now!' she shouted, each word punctuated by a slap of her palm on the desk. 'And release that picture to the media. I want all of London hunting these bastards down by lunchtime.'

AZRAEL WATCHED THE village burn. Deep in the Amazon rainforest, she stood atop a hill peeking above the canopy and saw the darkly dressed men creep between the wooden huts, splashing petrol around like teenage boys with their first bottles of cologne. With a 'whoomph', the first building went up in flames. Then another, and another, until the homes created a ring of fire. Azrael heard the screams above the crack and pop of the blaze, but she'd already become accustomed to the soundtrack accompanying slaughter, tuning it out like an irritating song on the radio.

She assumed this all had something to do with money, which seemed to be such a force amongst humans that it could drive them to kill. Somebody in one of those huts would tell her soon enough. It was all so predictable.

Azrael had done as Death suggested and looked into humanity's history. She didn't know what he was talking about. It was horror after horror. Where did you want to start? The Spanish Inquisition? Salem witch trials? To fight one world war could be considered unfortunate, to fight two seemed like carelessness. Sure, they'd knocked out a few nice paintings and written some catchy tunes, but did that make up for the innumerable terrors they'd inflicted upon each other? This was a failed project. Wouldn't it be better to wipe the slate clean and start again? To rebalance the scales of reality? This planet needed a break; to be given time to heal.

Were there others somewhere thinking the same thing? Another Famine, War, and Conquest? Azrael would look for them. But now, the flames below were dying down. She would need to greet a new intake of souls.

DEATH AND EMMA found a small coffee shop on a road just off Baker Street. While Death ordered the coffees at the counter, Emma found a table near the window and set up a new email account on her phone.

'Your password is "Penfold",' she said as Death placed a flat white on the table in front of her. 'I don't know how you've got this far in life without an email address.'

'I'm not a very online person,' replied Death.

'Looking at your phone, I'm not surprised.'

Death did have an email address, but b1llyjoelfan@yahoo.com wouldn't keep with the air of sophistication he was trying to maintain. Everyone had an embarrassing email address when they were younger, didn't they? Still, it was an excuse to spend some more time with Emma, and Death thought that time spent with her was better than time spent without.

They drank their coffees quietly for a moment, Death's mind racing, trying to think of something to talk about. Was this how most human interaction worked? One or both of them grasping for conversation starters? It was Emma who broke the silence.

'Can I ask what you do? For a living, I mean.'

'That's rather forward,' Death replied. Emma shrugged.

'I'm curious. What do you do that allows you to go looking for the headquarters of a kids' TV show character on a Wednesday morning?'

'I'm between jobs.'

'Sorry, I shouldn't have asked.'

'No, it's fine. I'd been doing the last job for a long, long time. It was time for a change.'

'What are you going to do next?'

'I don't have a clue.' Death sipped his cappuccino. When he lowered the cup, a small peak of foam had settled on the end of his nose.

'Let me get that,' Emma said. Before Death could reply, she'd picked up a napkin and removed the

141

milk in one smooth movement. 'Sorry. Force of habit.'

'No, don't apologise. It's a long time since someone looked out for me. Why did you become a nurse?'

'The money and the glamour,' Emma said with a tired smile. 'It's good to have a purpose. You know, when you wake up, and by the time you've gone to bed you've made a little difference to the world.'

'I thought I'd been put here for a purpose. It might be to act as a cautionary tale to others.'

Death looked out of the window at the world rushing past. All these people with somewhere to be. Here he was, having coffee on a midweek morning, something so alien to him, and it surprised him how... well... normal it felt. Steve Newman was a normal guy who did normal things. He wanted it to continue.

'Are you doing anything for the rest of the day?' he asked, as a curious hollow feeling carved itself into his stomach. Death had never been nervous in his previous life. He'd had no need. He didn't care for it now.

'Well, I was planning on breaking into the Blue Peter garden later on, but apart from that I'm free. Why?'

'I was just wondering whether you wanted to hang out?' Emma smiled.

'That sounds great.'

CARROLL'S MINI MOTORED through the London streets just below the speed limit as he tried to follow Sam's instructions to drive naturally. Anne had won the battle for the passenger seat while Sam folded himself up like a deckchair in the back.

'So, what's the plan?' Sam asked.

'To be honest, this is about as far as I'd got,' Carroll replied with a nervous laugh.

After only a few hours locked in that small, sense-depriving cell, the world threatened to overwhelm Anne with its sound and fury. She closed her eyes to shut it out, but all it did was return her to the narrow, windowless box beneath the ground.

'Where's this research you talked about?' she said, opening her eyes.

'I've hidden it in the toilet cistern of a Pret A Manger.'

'Well, let's go there for a start, shall we?'

Sam craned his neck, trying to get a view out of the windscreen. 'How long before they notice we're gone?'

'It wouldn't surprise me if they're already looking for us.'

'We need to dump this car.'

'Mini-Jim? I still haven't paid the loan off for him yet.'

'If they have a record of this car, which I'm sure they do, they'll be able to track us through ANPR.'

'ANPR?'

'Automatic Number Plate Recognition.' Sam pointed at a CCTV camera looking down from a building at the corner where two roads met. 'Once they've got an eye on this car, they can follow us wherever we go. That must be how they found us last night.'

'Where do we go afterwards?' asked Carroll. 'What do we even do with my data?'

Anne sighed. It had been a long week, and it was only Wednesday. When this was over, and if she was still a free woman, she'd find a nice quiet job in an office. Maybe in accountancy. She'd talked to an accountant at a party once and he seemed dull. She didn't know much about careers in financial services, but she was sure there were fewer opportunities for being tortured than there were in her current occupation.

'I know somewhere safe we can go. They'll be able to help us there,' she said, wondering at the same time whether it was fair to bring Dave into this. But what other choice did they have?

Soon, Carroll pulled up outside the sandwich shop. Sam didn't like the location on a busy main road, but there was nothing he could do. Carroll moved to turn the engine off, but Sam signalled him to stop.

'No, I'll go in. You keep the engine running.'

Carroll's hand returned to the steering wheel. 'It's the second cubicle from the left. A little plastic penguin,' he said, adding, 'It's all I had to hand. I was working in a time frame.'

Anne stepped out onto the pavement to let Sam out of the back seat. 'Anything else while I'm in there?' he asked.

'I could murder a sandwich,' Anne replied. 'Nothing fancy, just a ham and cheese.'

'I'd love a coffee,' said Carroll. 'You can use my loyalty card.'

Sam shook his head and slammed the door shut.

DAVE WAS PRONE on the living room floor, staring dead-eyed at the television screen, skipping from show to show. Mel, legs pulled up beneath her on the sofa, looked up from the laptop as he began a second circuit of the channels.

'Why don't you do something constructive?' she asked, irritation coating her words.

'I'm sad,' Dave replied.

'Too sad to do anything?'

'Remember when I realised, in Aliens, Ripley put Jonesy in a cattery and told him she'd be back in a few weeks and they never saw each other again?'

144

'You were inconsolable for a week.'

'Yeah, well, I feel worse now.' Dave's head flopped over to look at Melanie. 'What are you doing?'

'I thought one of us should look for another job.'

'So soon? Take some time to wallow. I am.'

'I never would've guessed.'

'Have you found anything?'

Melanie pointed to the screen. 'This one here is to analyse digital sector throughput engagement and segmentation.'

'I understand what all those words mean in isolation,' Dave said, 'but putting them together in that order has rendered them all meaningless. Nothing in finance administration?'

Melanie shook her head. 'The problem is, when UberSystems Tower disappeared, so did a lot of jobs. We flooded the market with competitors who are more qualified than us.'

'I apologise for not considering the economic repercussions of exorcising the restless spirits of a death cult.'

'Well, you'll know for next time.'

Dave turned his head back to the television. He needed to get a job. London was an expensive city and capitalism was a harsh mistress. And no matter how left-wing Gary claimed to be, there'd be trouble if Dave couldn't pay the rent and keep him in Peperamis.

'But when you *have* exorcised the restless spirits of a death cult, or destroyed a nest of vampire temps, it's hard to go back to scanning documents and processing customer withdrawals.'

'Why don't you go freelance?' Melanie asked. Dave turned back to her.

'What do you mean?'

'I watch a lot of those shows on the lifestyle channels where they explore haunted places. There are loads of them. They could hire you to investigate and de-haunt them.'

Dave pushed himself up onto his elbows. 'I have always wanted to be my own boss. I could get a van. And a talking dog.'

'Let's not get carried away, but maybe Death and Anne could go into business with you. You've already got an office.'

For the first time since his conversation with Azrael, Dave felt a twinge of optimism. He barely noticed the pulsing beat of the music heralding the one o'clock news on the television.

'New images released by the Ministry of Defence show three suspects fleeing from UberSystems Tower minutes before its destruction,' said the news anchor. Dave's full attention was now on the screen and the grainy image of three people on it.

'Hey! That bloke looks just like — '

The anchor replaced the photo. Dave fumbled for the remote control, rewound and hit pause. It was eerie to see himself on the television.

'Are they saying what I think they're saying?' asked Melanie.

'That we're wanted for the disappearance of UberSystems Tower? It sounds like it.'

Melanie's mobile phone rang on the arm of the sofa. The colour drained from her face. 'It's my dad. He's going to be so angry with me.'

'Don't answer it!' Dave yelled. 'They might triangulate the signal, or whatever, and find us.'

'It's probably best to let it go through to voicemail, anyway,' Melanie agreed. 'What do we do?'

'We need to find Death and Anne.'

They heard Gary's bedroom door open in the hallway. Dave pressed a button on the remote control and a dull documentary about tractors replaced the image of his face. Gary walked into the living room, beaming from ear-to-ear.

'As you know, I have little time for the mainstream media, but I channel-hop from time to time, to keep myself in the loop. You'll never guess what I've just seen.'

'It's not what it looks like. It's all a big misunderstanding,' Dave said.

Gary nodded. 'Oh, yeah. Of course it is. So how did you do it?'

'We didn't do anything,' Melanie protested.

'You didn't?' replied Gary. 'Well, why didn't you say?'

'But I just—' Dave blustered. Gary held up a hand, cutting him off.

'Remember, I like her.'

The doorbell's cheery two-tone chime shut Gary up.

'Is that the police already?' Melanie asked.

'I'll go down,' Gary said, heading for the door.

'Don't answer it!' Dave hissed.

'If you're as dangerous as the news report claims you are, they'll have spotters and snipers in the houses opposite with infra-red gunsights,' Gary explained. 'They'll know we're in here and have all the exits covered. The game's up. Would you rather we dealt with this calmly, or have them storm the flat with machine guns and stun grenades?'

'Actually, the second option sounds pretty cool,' Dave said. Gary shook his head.

'Do you know how hard it is to get a security deposit back when there's been a teargassing in the hallway?'

'Dave? Are you in there?' a woman's voice called from the front garden.

'That sounds like Anne,' Dave said, frowning. He ducked down and waddled over to the window. Parting the curtain with a finger, he peered over the

147

windowsill down onto the porch below. Anne was staring back up at him with two men Dave didn't recognise standing either side of her. She waved.

'Can we come in? We've had a hell of a morning.'
Dave turned back to Gary. 'Put the kettle on.'

ANNE, SAM AND Dr Carroll had dumped the car under some arches that Sam said were popular with car thieves. If they were lucky, it was being stripped for parts while Anne explained a high-level government conspiracy to Dave, Melanie and Gary over tea and biscuits.

'I bloody knew it,' Gary muttered, shaking his head.

'You knew that the government was funding research into wormholes to parallel worlds?' asked Dave.

'Well, *something* shady was going on,' Gary said with as much of a shrug as he could manage, squeezed as he was between Dave and Melanie on the sofa. Sam stood by the window, keeping a close eye on the street below, while Carroll and Anne had snagged the armchairs. Anne shifted in her seat. A rummage behind the cushion produced a games controller, a signed picture of Alan Shearer and what might've once been a chocolate bar. The usual detritus of the life of a twenty-something male, she thought. One day they'll grow up and discover storage solutions.

'So, you work with Dave?' Gary asked.

'Yes,' Anne replied. 'What has he told you we do?'

'He said it was something involving computers. To be honest, I get bored when he explains and switch off. I'm now guessing that's a cover story?'

Anne looked at Dave, who gave her permission to continue with a tiny nod.

'We work for a non-governmental organisation whose primary role is to investigate paranormal activity and help the souls of the dead pass on to the other side.'

While Gary took a moment to process this information, Anne saw Sam look over from the window. Another difficult conversation lay ahead.

'Fair enough.' Gary pointed at Carroll, who had cracked open a Custard Cream and was scraping the filling off with his teeth. 'And this guy is a physicist?'

'So he tells me.'

'And him over there is a copper?'

'Yes.'

'We've got the makings of one hell of a dinner party.' Gary turned to Dave. 'You were at UberSystems Tower when it disappeared?'

'We were,' Dave said.

'I can't believe you didn't tell me, I thought we were friends. I shared my Peperamis with you.'

Dave rolled his eyes. 'We are friends.'

'What happened?'

'It was sucked into another dimension by the ghosts of a death cult led by my old boss, Conrad West.'

'And that tore a hole in the fabric of space-time that this physicist guy has been exploiting for his research?' Gary asked. 'Do you understand the abuse I'm going to get at the Truther Symposium when they find out this has been going on right under my nose?'

'You're taking this all rather well, Gary,' said Anne. Gary shrugged.

'Rich people get up to some weird shit. You should hear what Elon Musk does with a particle accelerator and a ouija board on the weekends. So, what are you going to do now? I'm rather upset I'm sat in a room of six people and I'm the only one not wanted by the government.'

Sam reached into his pocket and produced the small plastic penguin. 'Hypothetically, if I wanted to leak top secret government research papers onto the internet, what would be the best way of doing that? Anne says that you might be the person who'd know.'

Gary gave Sam a devilish grin. 'Now it's my time to shine.'

GARY TOOK THE memory stick from Sam and disappeared into his bedroom. He demanded complete privacy but explained to them what he intended to do. Using a special browser, he'd use The Onion Router, or Tor, which was a way to route internet traffic through several servers on its way to its destination. They all looked blankly at him. He sighed.

'It's like driving to lots of safe houses and switching cars and clothes before arriving where you want to go,' he said. Everybody nodded this time. 'Then, using encrypted communications, we can upload the documents and pass them to the media.'

Satisfied Gary knew what he was doing, all the others could do was wait. Once Sam had persuaded Dave and Melanie that the government couldn't trace them from a phone call, they retreated to his bedroom to have an uncomfortable conversation with her dad. Carroll perched himself on an armchair to watch daytime television. Anne went into the kitchen to find Sam stood at the sink, chipping away at strata of hardened food fused to a dinner plate.

'You're taking your life into your own hands, there,' Anne said. Sam dropped various cups and bowls into the bubbly water to soak.

'I can't just sit and do nothing.'

'That's all we can do.' Sam grabbed a scrunched-up tea towel from the sideboard and rubbed his hands, putting it back when he realised they were stickier than before he'd used it.

'How long do you think it'll take to get some kind of response?' he asked, wiping his hands on his thighs. Anne shrugged.

'Gary said it could be a few minutes, or a few hours.'

Sam opened and closed cupboard doors, scanning the contents of each with trained eyes.

'What are you looking for?' Anne asked.

'Some booze. If we're stuck here, we might as well have a drink,' Sam replied, reaching to the back of the cupboard beneath the sink. His face lit up as his hand wrapped around a bottle. It dropped when he read the label. 'Chilli vodka? I didn't expect these lads to be single malt drinkers, but come on.'

Anne grabbed two glasses from the draining board and carried them over to the kitchen table. 'Beggars can't be choosers.'

They sat at the little table. Sam poured generous shots into each glass. They raised them and threw them down their necks in one.

'Actually, that's not too—' At that moment, Sam lost all ability to speak. Simultaneously, Anne had an idea what it might be like to gargle with molten lava. Her throat burned raw and her face brightened with the colour and heat of a red supergiant star. As she wiped tears from her eyes, it delighted her that the feeling soon subsided to a mere inferno in her belly.

'Another?' Sam gasped. Anne nodded and held her glass out.

When he could form sentences again, Sam asked, 'Do you want to talk about last night?'

'What about it?' Anne wheezed.

'You don't have to put a brave face on. It's not every day you're bundled into a car by special forces and held in an underground cell in a top-secret military installation.'

'I'm fine, but thanks for looking out for me.' Though she was more than capable of handling herself, it was nice to know that there was someone in her corner.

'Any time. Now that's out of the way, can we talk about the weird stuff earlier?'

'What weird stuff, specifically?' Anne asked.

'What you said about ghosts. You believe that?'

'What do you think happens when you die?'

'That doesn't matter. Let's just cut to the cheese, do you think you see dead people?'

'Cut to what?'

'The cheese.'

'That's not the expression.'

'Yes, it is.'

'Then explain the meaning.'

'The cheese course is at the end of a meal, so it means you're jumping to the important part of a subject without wasting time.'

Anne gave a supportive smile and patted Sam's hand. 'Let's come back to that, but have you never contemplated what happens when you die?'

Sam opened his mouth to answer when Gary walked into the room.

'There's a couple of great episodes of Buffy on that drive,' Gary said.

'Shouldn't you be working on those files?' Sam asked, all business once again.

'Relax, they're uploading. Oh, have we got the chilli vodka out?'

Gary grabbed a glass from a cupboard and three Peperamis from the fridge. He passed one each to Sam and Anne as he took a seat at the table. Anne examined the long foil package before sliding it into her jacket pocket.

'I'll save mine for later.'

'Me too,' said Sam.

THE FIGHT WAS over. The dead and dying littered the desert landscape, blood and sand mixing into a thick, dark cocktail. In the deep blue sky above, vultures pinwheeled, impatient for feeding time to start. Azrael wandered the battlefield, shaking her head at the loss of life. With no idea what to do, the ghosts of the vanquished followed her like lost puppies.

'Excuse me,' one of them dared to say.

'Yes?'

'What happened?'

'You're dead.' She told him, tired of sugarcoating the truth.

'How?'

Azrael laughed. It was harsh and devoid of humour. 'You're joking, right?' She pointed fingers. 'He shot you. That one shot him over there. This guy, I don't know what he thought he was doing with those hand grenades. Yeah, don't turn away, I'm talking about you. So here we are. No doubt you're all considering the consequences of your actions. I know some of you will be surprised that, whatever your religion, ethnicity, or place of birth, you've all ended up at the same place.'

Azrael looked at their frightened faces. Enemies minutes before, fear and confusion now united them. It occurred to her that the only place different people could get along would be the afterlife. Only then could they realise they were all equal. It was like that film, The Breakfast Club, only in this case eternity is the metaphorical school library where they can talk about their feelings until the end of time.

History was cyclical. The dinosaurs rose before being wiped out by an asteroid. Humanity had taken their place, had their chance, and failed too. Look at what they were doing to the planet. Stripping it of its resources, replacing them with poisons, stinking up the atmosphere. Don't judge their actions? It was impossible not to. They made the same mistakes again and again. It was time to give something else a go. With nobody around to poach them or destroy their habitat, maybe it was time for gorillas to evolve, or let the dolphins have a crack. She looked down at a corpse at her feet. Left here, it would break down, feeding the earth. Now times that by seven billion. It would be a world reborn.

That idea sparked a new one, then another. *This must be imagination,* Azrael reflected. Notions splintered in her mind's eye, taking her speculations down new avenues. Her head buzzed with infinite possibilities. When the train of thought arrived at its station, she understood everything. They called her Azrael, but that's not who she was. Nor was she Famine, or War, or Conquest. She was so much more. There were no others for her to find. They had sent four in the past, but now there only needed to be one to carry out the work.

She would not wait.

She was Oblivion.

SYED NAZIM DROVE along the Westway, delighted that the traffic was flowing freely for once. He didn't normally drive into the capital, but he only had one meeting. It was outside the Congestion Charge Zone, and the car needed a run.

Syed worked analysing digital section throughput engagement and segmentation. Learning on his first day on the job that he didn't understand what that involved, he soon realised nobody else in the company did either. And none of them wanted to be the one who looked an idiot by saying they didn't understand. So he attended meetings like the one he'd had that morning, and came out with some buzzwords that made the other attendees nod their heads sagely. As London rolled beneath him, Syed was considering how he could write the day up into a report when the atmosphere in front of his Volvo ripped open.

Roadworks were the most common inconvenience he'd encountered on London's roads, but anomalies in four-dimensional space-time were rarer. The anomaly glowed faintly; a perfect circle carved into the universe. If you'd asked Syed to describe what a wormhole looked like, the portal in front of him would be an excellent match. Then, he realised he was overthinking things, but before he could hit the brakes, he passed the lip of the tunnel that led around the back of reality.

AFTER AN ACCIDENT, people often say that a car came out of nowhere. Here, it literally did. At least, that's what the witnesses later told the police officer, who dutifully wrote it down in her notebook.

It was late afternoon on a beautiful spring day and Piccadilly Circus was like - well - Piccadilly Circus. Backpacked exchange students sat on the steps leading up to Eros while tourists photographed the giant screen wrapped around the buildings at the northern end, under which tired PA's ran into Boots to buy their lunch.

The air above their heads crackled, the atmosphere turning heavy as if a storm was gathering. Then, without warning, the sky gave birth to a Volvo with above average mileage and a slippy clutch. It appeared about twenty feet above everybody's heads and seemed to hover there momentarily, which came as a surprise to all, particularly gravity. The car, with Syed still inside, dropped to the ground and crashed nose-first into the road that cut through the junction. The airbags exploded, burying Syed's face. The car tipped back onto its wheels, its front end crumpled, shedding wing mirrors and chrome and then rocking back and forth on the suspension. Cars and buses swerved to avoid the Volvo and the debris, some clipping the vehicle next to them and the barriers lining the side of the road.

The confusion died down and all traffic, both pedestrian and engine-powered, froze for a moment. Then everyone burst into applause. Surely this must be the greatest advertisement for the Swedish car company's safety features ever conceived. When nobody came forward to take credit for the feat, the applause petered out.

'Maybe we should call an ambulance?' a voice in the crowd asked. Then the driver's door opened, and Syed waved weakly to the people running towards him to help.

Before he could get out of the car, a hundred phones were uploading the footage to the cloud.

THE ART GALLERY buzzed with activity, visitors moving from room to room through the tall wood-framed doorways as small children slid on the parquet flooring. Death wasn't sure why he'd chosen to bring Emma to this place, but according to the films he'd watched over the years, this is where humans came when they wanted to look sophisticated and sensitive.

He cast a lazy eye over the pictures hanging on the surrounding walls in the seventeenth century room. He'd met the subject of every single painting staring back at him. Some of them had been dispatched by the occupant of another canvas just along the wall.

The crowds of tourists parted, and Death's gaze settled on Emma. He studied her as intently as she did the portrait of a Puritan preacher hanging in front of her, wondering what was going on inside her mind. It was one of the most interesting things about the human experience. You could know someone for a thousand years, but you wouldn't learn everything about them. Everybody had some part that remained secret, locked away from everyone else. Maybe even from themselves. That was where both the fun and the heartbreak was, trying to solve that mystery.

Emma looked over and smiled. Walking back towards Death, she carried herself in a relaxed way, as if she was lighter, the weight of the world off her shoulders temporarily.

'Enjoying it?' Death asked. Emma nodded.

'They're wonderful, aren't they? I stare into their eyes and think about what's going on behind them.'

'It was the Age of Enlightenment,' Death replied. 'Are they contemplating the sovereignty of reason over superstition, or are they meditating on whether they left the loom on when they left the house?'

Emma pointed at a picture of a man wearing a large ruff and a pointed beard. He glowered back at them. 'That guy is definitely wondering where that weird smell is coming from.'

They both laughed. Death enjoyed the way it felt, the endorphins flooding his body. A security guard hushed them quiet.

'Do you want to get out of here?' Emma asked. Before Death could reply, she took him by the hand and pulled him in the exit's direction. He was very aware that she didn't let go.

ANNE HOPPED FROM one news channel to another, but the top story was always the same: Anne Mitchell. She didn't like to be the centre of attention at the best of times, let alone have the world's media speculating about her motives. With little else to go on, newsreaders, reporters and pundits talked endlessly about the photograph and its subjects' obvious criminal tendencies. Anne couldn't help but take it personally.

Gary joined the others gathered in the living room. They all looked at him expectantly.

'Well?' Dave asked. Gary put his hands in his pockets and rocked back and forth on his heels.

'Nobody's got back to me about the files yet, but it could be because they're all busy with this, ironically.' Gary nodded at the television.

Anne was glad to see the news cycle had moved on. Now they were showing CCTV film of a sensible family hatchback driving along the Westway and disappearing into thin air. Then she was looking at unsteady phone footage of Piccadilly Circus, unsure where she should focus her attention until the same hatchback appeared in mid-air without warning and crashed into the road below.

'This footage came in earlier this afternoon,' the news anchor said over the film before the report cut back to the studio. The anchor, confusion furrowing his brow, stared at the screen embedded into his desk.

'Reports are coming in about an incident at the London Eye,' he said. 'I think we can go to Riverside live now.'

The picture changed again to a view of the old County Hall building. 'You'll notice that the London Eye is conspicuous by its absence,' the anchor continued. And it was true. Where the four-hundred feet tall structure should have been revolving there was nothing but empty air. 'The question is, is this the same phenomenon that affected UberSystems Tower? Let's go to our correspondent Sophie Bailey, who has some developments in Trafalgar Square. What's going on there, Sophie?'

The television image switched to a news reporter who was trying to keep the bafflement she was feeling from showing on camera. Over her shoulder, the familiar view of Nelson's Column stood proudly in the centre of the square. What was less familiar was the perfect circle of the London Eye propped up against the granite column beneath the statue of Nelson, like a hula hoop left by an absent-minded giant.

'Your guess is as good as mine, Simon,' Sophie said down the camera. 'Witnesses say the London Eye appeared, toppled over and ended up in the position you see now. The police have evacuated the area and are now trying to figure out how to get to the sightseers trapped in the thirty-two passenger capsules. When I contacted a representative of the London Mayor about the situation, she said it would make a day out in London more efficient. When I explained that it wasn't a joke, she withdrew her previous statement and said something I can't broadcast.'

Anne realised that this was one of those handful of moments in a lifetime where the world around her was changing forever.

'What's causing this?' she asked.

'Don't get cross, but I think I may have fractured reality,' Carroll replied. 'I didn't understand how bad it was.'

Sam leaned forward in his chair. 'Is this going to continue?'

'Yeah, if it carries on like this, then reality will swallow itself whole.'

'That's no good for me,' said Gary. 'I've got tickets to a gig next week.'

'But the government must know what's going on, right?' Mel said. 'They must have their top men working on it.'

'Unfortunately, their top man has spent the afternoon watching repeats of Bargain Hunt,' Dave said, nodding towards Carroll.

'Okay, is there any way we can stop this?' Mel asked.

Carroll nodded. 'There's a device called the Interdimensional Generator Using Multiverse-Mapping Integration, or Thingummy for short—'

'The Thingummy?' Sam repeated.

'I know, but they axed the department in charge of naming things in the last round of budget cuts. Anyway, we use it to open and stabilise the portals. There might be a way of reversing the effects and closing those wormholes.'

'That's great,' Anne said. 'What do you need?'

'My research notes, a laptop, and a cheese sandwich. I haven't eaten all day.'

'We can do the first two,' Dave said. 'What about the third?'

'There's something in the fridge that recently became cheese,' Gary suggested.

'There's one problem,' said Carroll.

Anne knew there always was. 'What's that?'

'I can't remotely upload the code changes to the Thingummy. We need to go to the project headquarters.'

'Of course you do. Why should this be easy? It's somewhat of an issue when we're the most wanted people in the country,' Sam said.

'Where is the Thingummy?' asked Dave.

'Canary Wharf tube station.'

Sam looked at Gary, Dave, and Mel. 'I don't suppose any of you have a car?'

'I don't see the point of owning a car in London,' Gary said.

'How do we get across East London with no transport?' Anne asked.

'I think I might know someone,' Sam said. 'I need to make a phone call.'

Everyone nodded in approval. Then Sam added, 'Could I borrow someone's phone, please? An angry tool of the establishment stamped on mine last night.'

DEATH AND EMMA had enjoyed dinner in a small restaurant on a quiet street. Death had come across it several years ago when a diner suffered a heart attack during dessert. Since then, he'd wanted to visit but never had the opportunity for obvious reasons. The atmosphere seemed nice, even with a corpse at one table. He remembered the diner had recommended the goat's cheese soufflé from beyond the grave. Tonight, while Emma had chosen the mussels, Death ordered cheesecake for each course because he realised he was an adult and could do whatever he wanted.

Now, sitting with a drink on the south bank of the Thames on a warm spring evening was one of life's simple pleasures, Death thought. Partly because you couldn't see the south bank. He looked down on the twilight glimmer of the city lights sparkling on the dark water, the curved dome of St Paul's Cathederal rising behind.

'Did you know Samuel Pepys watched the Great Fire of London from this pub?' Emma asked. Death smiled as he watched the ebb and flow of the crowds walking along the length of the river.

'I think I heard that somewhere.'

Their knees touched and Death felt a little hiccup of excitement in his chest. Was the contact deliberate on Emma's part, or an accident? Sweat pin-pricked his brow, his mouth was dry, and worry hung heavy in his stomach. How did humans get to a point where they realised they wanted to spend the rest of their lives together without collapsing with anxiety and dehydration?

A young couple in the street below caught his attention. The boy was trying to hold a bored girl's interest. He envied these people's ancestors. You knew where you stood when rescuing future partners from evil wizards. It was a lot less awkward than trying to have interesting opinions about your favourite films.

'Can I tell you something? I didn't just go to Baker Street this morning to visit a postbox,' Emma said. 'I was hoping I might see you there.'

Death's heart rate quickened. 'Really?'

'It's hard to meet people with similar interests in a city this size. It's too easy to slip into being alone.'

'Being alone isn't the worst thing,' Death said with a sad smile.

'Yeah, but it's not the best.'

Death hadn't even noticed that they'd moved closer to each other, leaning on the table, their elbows touching. Is this what attraction was? Small actions and tiny responses until they reached a tipping point, and the feelings were obvious to both parties? Some unknown force was pulling him towards Emma as an equal and opposite energy pushed her in his direction. They kissed. Only a couple of days ago Death didn't even have lips and now look at him, snogging up a storm. He thought he was doing it right, but he didn't have much to go on. As long as you didn't think about how weird the concept was, he understood why humans enjoyed it. Knowing that somebody else liked you was a fine thing.

'I'm sorry. Am I interrupting something?' Azrael cast a shadow over the table. She looked preoccupied, so much going on behind those eyes.

'Hello, Azrael. How are you?' Death asked.

'I am well. I now have clarity of purpose.'

'That's splendid news,' Death said, and he meant it. 'Oh, sorry. I should do introductions. Azrael, this is Emma. Emma, this is Azrael.' Azrael nodded to Emma, acknowledging her. Emma smiled back.

'Lovely to meet you,' she said to Azrael. 'How do you know Steve?'

'Work,' Death cut in before Azrael answered, then to Azrael, 'What have you been up to?'

'Not as much as you, obviously,' Azrael said, looking from Death to Emma and back again, raising her eyebrows. 'I sat atop a mountain. The air was so clear I saw the curvature of the earth. From the peak, the world stretched out before me like some beautiful blanket, a patchwork of a myriad of landscapes, each one unique—'

'We looked at some paintings,' Death said.

'Ate some cheesecake,' Emma joined in.

'Yeah, ate some cheesecake. It was nice.'

'Yeah.'

Azrael looked cross. She was trying to say something important, and they'd broken her stride. 'Imagination is not something that comes easy to me,' she continued, 'but as I took in the majesty of creation, I could almost see how lovely this planet would be without them.'

'Who's "them"?' asked Emma. Azrael's eyes flicked over to her and back again, ignoring the irritating interruption.

'We should allow the world to start again, to rebuild and regenerate,' Azrael said to Death. 'Something else would come along, eventually. Something better. I'm prepared to wait and then to guide them.'

Death's unease grew as he looked into Azrael's eyes, and something more dangerous replaced the irritation. 'And how are you going to do that?'

'There's a crack in the universe.'

'Yes, I remember you saying.'

'I will pull the world inside of itself. You will witness the birth of something new.'

'Now look, Azrael—'

'Azrael is not my name. I am Oblivion.'

Before Death answered, Oblivion slipped through a gap in reality and disappeared. Emma jumped to her feet and looked over the table.

'Well, where the bloody hell did she go?'

'I'm sorry, Emma, but I'm going to have to leave,' Death said. 'I think she's going to do something rash.'

'Who is she? An ex-girlfriend?' asked Emma. 'Not jealous, by the way.'

'No, it's nothing like that. I'm just worried for her. I'll call you.'

'Nuh-huh. I'm coming with you. It sounds like you might need my help. Where are we going?'

Death remembered his conversation with Anne and Dave the day before. There was an energy in the city, the likes of which they had felt only once before.

'To UberSystems Tower. Or where it used to be, at least.'

OBLIVION RETURNED TO UberSystems Plaza and the foundations of UberSystems Tower. She looked up at the forest of buildings around her. The structures were so brutal, so ugly, so *human*. Not to worry. Soon nature would reclaim this land, burying the buildings under lush greenery.

Worlds intersected where she stood, a spider's web of universes, and just as delicate. She wrapped her hands around thick fibres of reality, trailing through dimensions like vines. With effort she could drag one over the other, ripping them apart, and those gaps full of unreality through which wormholes travelled would scour the face of the earth. Then the actual work would begin.

She did not underestimate the magnitude of her task. Billions of souls, all equal for the first time in their history. No oppression, or anger, or hate. She would need to visit each one.

Oblivion pulled and worlds rubbed against each other, the air crackling with a special friction. She felt dizzy, as if the world was spinning beneath her. The sky shimmered, teasing at what existed behind the veil between this world and the next. A spark flashed near to where Oblivion stood, and a lightning bolt hung in the air. It extended, glowing white and blue, following the edges of where the worlds met, until the night resembled a 3D puzzle box in need of a solution.

WHAT THE FUCK is that?' asked Kelvin, looking up at the blazing sky while trying to keep the car on the road. 'Is this something to do with your parallel worlds, doc?'

'I'd say it would be a massive coincidence if it wasn't,' replied Sam from the passenger seat.

'Yes, it seems likely,' Carroll said, crushed between Dave and Anne on the back seat. 'Can you see where it's coming from?'

'It's UberSystems Tower,' Dave said with resignation.

Sam had called Kelvin, one of only two men Sam trusted and the only one with a car. When he'd arrived, they'd explained the situation to him. Luckily, Kelvin had read several popular science books on quantum physics and had watched Sliding Doors twice.

'You won't turn us in?' Sam asked him. Kelvin shook his head.

'I've known you for five years, guv, and this would be out of character. Between the job and your box sets, I couldn't see where you'd find time to plan the theft of a train.'

Sam turned to Anne. 'I have other hobbies.'

Carroll had written the code changes to reverse the Thingummy, and they'd agreed that they would help to get Carroll into the research facility beneath Canary Wharf. Mel and Gary were to stay at the flat to monitor the online part of the operation and, in Gary's case, because it was almost teatime.

'I should check out what's going on at UberSystems Plaza,' Dave said.

'Why you?' Anne asked.

Dave folded his arms in a sulk. 'Because I always bloody well end up at that place. Why change the habit of a lifetime? Of course, I'm going to miss my one opportunity to go into a secret underground government research lab.'

'I'm going with Carroll,' Sam said. 'It's my job to find those missing passengers and I'm going to finish it.'

'Me too,' said Anne.

Kelvin looked in the rear-view mirror. 'I guess that means I'm with you, Darren.'

'Dave.'

The decision was made. The occupants of the car sat in silence, assured in their purpose. Then Dave cleared his throat. 'Is there any chance we can put the siren on?'

IT HAD BEEN half an hour since Oblivion had started to destroy all human life, and it disappointed her how little progress she'd made. Still, mass genocide was a marathon, not a sprint. Oblivion was young and had the stamina to see it through to the end.

But something seemed to be wedged between here and the next world. If she could remove that, her work would be so much easier. She located where it was caught up in the fabric of the universe, then squeezed until it gave way and the blockage popped out.

UberSystems Tower crashed down out of nothingness. With a mind-bending creak of metal and a shrill scream of glass, it toppled and crashed into the buildings surrounding Oblivion with a force felt as far as Wembley. It lay across roofs like a crystal tree felled by the same absent-minded giant who'd abandoned the London Eye.

Oblivion sighed with relief. 'That's better.'

LORRAINE ARDEN WATCHED the developing situation on her office television along with her special advisers at M.O.D.U.L.E. She turned to Captain Mills, stood at ease to the side of her desk.

'Captain, I'd like you to go down there and look into this personally.' Mills snapped to attention.

'Yes, ma'am.'

'Dr Carroll, Mitchell and Graves are mixed up in this and I want them brought here. If they were to fall down a flight of stairs or two on the way back, that wouldn't be the worst thing in the world.'

'Understood, ma'am.'

On the television, UberSystems Tower fell from the sky.

'That isn't anything to do with us, is it?' Arden asked the room.

WHEN THE TAXI driver was as close to the action as he was comfortable getting, he ordered Emma and Death out of the cab. With no other transport available, they set out on foot in the opposite direction of travel to the rest of the city's population.

A symphony of sirens filled the air as the emergency services once again headed towards the danger. There'd be cordons and barriers set up soon, but this part of London was a maze, making it easy enough to lose yourself among the passages and backstreets.

'What's happening?' Emma asked for the umpteenth time as Death poked his head around the corner of an alleyway. The street was deserted, so he took her hand and they ran to the shadows on the other side of the road.

Death sighed. Emma had followed him into potential jeopardy, possibly risking her life. She deserved more than cryptic statements and enigmatic gazes.

'I'm not who you think I am. I have a past,' he said.

'Everyone has baggage.'

'This is the full Louis Vuitton luggage set.'

'Is this anything to do with a beautiful and mysterious woman who seems to disappear into thin air? Still not jealous.'

Death took a deep breath. 'I was De—' It's always difficult to find the right time to have that serious conversation. Things get in the way. A phone call from a friend, or the commercial break during the show you're watching is over. That's life.

The thing getting in the way right now, was a bloody great building falling from the sky.

KELVIN'S CAR RACED along the empty road and mounted the pavement in front of Canary Wharf tube station. He pulled at the handbrake and threw the steering wheel to the right, forcing the car into a spin. Rubber peeled from the tyres, leaving thick black marks on the concrete slabs. When the car came to a rest, Kelvin let out a whoop of glee as his passengers fell out of the doors on either side.

The square was empty, the camera crews and journalists abandoning their posts. Sam could understand why. They were uncomfortably close to the lightning, the thick ropes of plasma and energy twisting up into the black sky and fanning out in all directions. The glass buildings reflected its light, bathing everything in a harsh blue-white glow.

The radio crackled into life. 'Any patrols near UberSystems Plaza? We have reports it's raining buildings there.'

'That'll be us,' Dave said to Kelvin. They headed back to the car, Kelvin sliding over the bonnet to get to the driver's side.

'That's not fair,' Sam muttered. 'I wanted to do that.'

With Dave gripping the grab handle above his head, Kelvin wheel-span the car and sped off towards the lightning. Sam shook his head.

'That boy's having far too much fun.'

'Come on,' Carroll said. 'We've got gateways to unknown realms to destroy.'

Anne, Sam and Carroll headed for the escalators down to the station entrance where a solitary soldier remained at his post.

'What's going on, Dr Carroll?' he asked. 'Is this the end of the world?'

Obviously, Carroll's fugitive status hadn't reached down here. That, or the nervous young man just didn't care. Carroll glanced down at his name badge. 'Not if I can get down there and stop it, Hughes.'

Hughes stepped aside to allow him to pass. 'Fill yer boots.'

'Thank you,' Carroll said, already descending the stationary escalator. Anne and Sam followed him down, before Sam turned back.

'You're not doing any good here, son,' he said to Hughes. 'Find something constructive to do. People are going to need help.'

'Yes, sir.' Hughes turned and ran off in a random direction, determined to do what Sam had ordered.

Sam rejoined Carroll and Anne as they were running through the open security barriers. Down another escalator, they were running along the platform when Anne cried out, 'My handbag!' and swerved towards the platform's edge.

Someone had propped her handbag up against the security glass and, once she'd checked the contents and Sam had looked at his watch, they continued to the door at the end of the platform. Carroll took his security card from a jacket pocket and held his breath. He pressed the card against the keypad. The light changed from red to green and the lock clicked open. Carroll let out a sigh of relief. The wheels of government administration had turned too slow to cancel his security clearance. He pulled the door open and led Anne and Sam down a dark corridor.

'I wish Kelvin was here,' Sam gasped.

'Would he have been of help?' asked Anne.

'No, I wish he was here instead of me and I was in the car.'

'This is the last set of stairs, I promise,' Carroll panted as they followed the winding staircase down to the dimly-lit control room, the only light coming from the television broadcast. Silhouetted against the glare of the screen, a lone figure sat at one terminal, typing away at the keyboard.

'Rose? What are you still doing here?'

Rose turned around. 'Never mind me, Dr Carroll. What are you doing here? Half the army is out looking for you.'

'I think they might have bigger fish to fry,' Carroll replied, pointing to the television screen.

'Yes, I've been monitoring the situation. All the known wormholes along with some brand new ones are open.'

'That's quicker than I calculated. There must be something we haven't accounted for.'

Carroll pulled a laptop from the messenger bag he had borrowed from Dave and took the seat next to Rose.

'I'm going to start reprogramming the Thingummy,' he said. 'If the wormholes are open, there's a chance you'll be able to get to the passengers.'

'How long have we got?' Sam asked, already climbing back up the stairs. Carroll looked at his watch and performed some calculations in his head.

'I'd say thirty minutes.' Sam groaned.

'Does that mean we have to start running again?'

A THICK LAYER of dust coated the streets around UberSystems Plaza, the white glow of the lightning turning the cityscape into something close to a Christmas scene, if you ignored the crushed cars and chunks of masonry laying in the road. The police were efficiently clearing the buildings around the impact zone, ordering everyone they came across to evacuate to a safe distance.

Death and Emma hid in the reception area of a small advertising company, crouched behind an air hockey table, waiting for the officers to move on.

'What were you going to tell me in the street before a thirty-storey building rudely interrupted us?' Emma asked. Death closed his eyes, a sensation he still hadn't got used to. It would be easier if he didn't look at her.

'What's your belief system?' he asked.

'What's that got to do with anything?' Emma replied, baffled.

'Just want to gauge how to pitch this.'

'I don't really give it much thought, day-to-day. I was raised Protestant, go to church at Christmas. Pretty standard.'

'I'm not human, or I became human only recently at least. I was born of chaos and pandemonium. I was the whisper on the lips of the damned. The dark companion who walked in the shadows of humanity's souls. I was Death.'

Death didn't mean to be so grandiose, but he was so used to saying it that way that he simply fell back into the groove.

'I'm sorry? Death?' Emma laughed. 'You mean like the Grim Reaper, with the scythe and hourglass and everything?'

'Yes, but I didn't have an hourglass and I'm not sure where the scythe is.'

Emma sat back against the table. 'I have to say, this is the weirdest way I've been rejected, and I was once dumped during a tandem parachute jump. That was an awkward ten thousand feet. Couldn't you say it's not you, it's me? Y'know, the classics?'

'I'm being serious.'

'That just freaks me out more.'

There was a commotion outside as a Vauxhall Astra rounded the corner at a dangerous speed. Its wheels kicked up a fog of vaporised concrete as two police officers jumped out of the way. With a flourish, the car came to a stop in a final, choking cloud. Kelvin jumped from the driver's side, waving his warrant card at the angry officers. Dave stumbled out.

'Sorry, sorry,' Kelvin said. 'Is everybody alright?'

'What the bloody hell are you playing at?' a uniformed sergeant asked.

'Got a little carried away,' Kelvin replied with an embarrassed grin.

'What are you doing here?'

'Come to lend a hand. We'll finish here and you guys can get back to the critical incident unit. Take the car.' Kelvin threw the keys to the sergeant who looked warily up at the skyscraper bridging the gap between office blocks further down the street.

'Fair enough,' he said. He and the other cop climbed into the car.

'Be careful. I was a little bit sick in the glove box,' Dave called after them.

'I know that whiny voice,' Death whispered to Emma. He peered over the top of the table to see the Astra receding into the distance as Dave and Kelvin brushed the dust from their clothes. He offered his hand to Emma, who ignored it. 'Come on. The idiot has landed.'

They exited the building and Death called out, 'Dave!'

Dave turned around. He smiled and walked over to his old friend.

'What are you doing here?'

'The usual,' replied Death. 'Saving the world. What about you?'

Dave shrugged. 'Same.'

'Will you tell me what's going on?' Emma asked.

'Emma, isn't it?' Dave said with a knowing grin. 'Well, we came here for the trans-dimensional wormholes, but we're staying for the giant lightning'n'shit.'

Kelvin arrived at Dave's shoulder. 'We need to get these civilians out of here.'

'They're friends of mine. In fact, they'll be able to help. He's my boss.'

Kelvin looked them up and down. 'Okay.'

'What's this about wormholes?' Emma asked.

'Oh, a secret government project has fractured reality by experimenting on wormholes and it's threatening to rip the world apart,' Dave said. 'Where's Azrael?'

Death pointed at the lightning.

'Did you know she fired me this morning?' Dave asked.

'She's calling herself Oblivion now,' Death replied.

'Doesn't sound like her mood's improved, then.'

'She told me she's going to destroy humanity. I'm guessing by using those wormholes.'

Dave sighed. 'Why do the pretty ones always turn out to be insane demons who want to bring about the end of the world?'

'It'll explain where that's come from.' Death nodded towards UberSystems Tower.

'Yeah, I thought we'd got rid of that.'

'Excuse me,' said Emma. 'Are you saying this is the end of the world?'

'Yes,' Death and Dave said in unison.

'You're rather calm about the whole thing.'

'This isn't our first rodeo,' Death said.

'Of course not,' said Emma, rolling her eyes. 'You're Death.'

'You told her?' Dave said, shocked.

'Does he tell everyone this?' Emma asked, faking a pout. 'I feel less special now.'

'SO, HOW DO WE STOP IT?' Kelvin shouted.

'No. I said he's Death, not deaf,' Emma replied.

'Oh, sorry,' said Kelvin, and repeated the question at a normal volume. 'So how do we stop it?'

Death looked at Dave. 'Any ideas?'

'We've got a guy who's working on closing the wormholes. This whole Angel of Death thing has mucked the plan up a bit, though.'

'I'm sorry, the angel of what?' Emma asked.

'Death,' Dave repeated.

'I thought you were Death?' Emma said to Death.

'No, I said I *was* Death. She's a replacement.'

'Seems a bit too keen, if you ask me.'

Kelvin tapped Dave on the shoulder. 'They've got footage of what's going on in there.'

On his phone was a news report showing the view from a drone hovering high above UberSystems Plaza. The gigantic bolt of lightning thrusted skyward, dwarfing the figure of Azrael, her arms stretched wide. Wielding that kind of power, how could they possibly defeat her?

'Just having a weapon of some sort would help,' Death muttered. Dave's face lit up.

'What happened to that flaming sword you had?'

'Oh, I left it in the boardroom at—' Death looked up at UberSystems Tower, then back to Dave. 'Do you think it's still there?'

'There's only one way to find out,' said Dave.

'How would we even get up there?'

'If we can make it to the roof of the building the top of the tower is resting on, then it's a quick climb.'

'Help!' a voice cried weakly from a car on the side of the road, its roof crushed by a boulder. Emma and Kelvin ran over. Kelvin pulled at the driver's door handle, but it was stuck fast.

'Don't worry. We'll get you out,' Kelvin told the occupant. Emma moved around the vehicle, looking for a way in.

'I can help,' she said. 'I'm a nurse.'

Kelvin knew he was out of his depth when it came to buildings falling out of the sky and lightning bursting out of the ground, but he could help a person trapped below a rock. He looked over at Death and Dave, then pointed at the lightning. 'Can you two handle that?'

'Yes,' Dave replied. Death's eyes followed Kelvin's finger to the vast streak of energy.

'Oh, I hadn't noticed that.'

'IF I EVER go below ground again, you have my permission to punch me in the face,' Sam said. Anne led him through the half-light of the tunnel, torch beams criss-crossing in front of them, towards the abandoned train.

As they trampled along the track in silence, the enveloping darkness made Sam's gaze turn inwards. The events of the day had stirred up memories, and some floated to the surface. He came to a halt.

'Something happened when I was a kid,' Sam said, speaking to the dark as much as to Anne.

'Pardon?'

'You asked me if anything happened to me I couldn't explain.'

'Yes, I did.' Sam started walking again, the urgency of the situation never far from his mind.

'My grandad, my dad's dad, died before I was born. He was a copper, too. My parents didn't talk about him. I'd seen no photographs. There'd been some falling out. I never asked why.

Anyway, one night I was playing in my bedroom, I was five or six, and I looked up and there was an old man sitting on my bed. I wasn't scared because I felt like I knew him. He had my father's eyes. Or, rather, my father had his eyes. He told me he was my grandad, Daniel. He asked me to tell my dad he was fine. Then he was gone.

'When I went downstairs and told my parents, they were naturally concerned. They asked me to describe the man I talked to, which I did. Then they got a photograph from a family reunion a few years before, and I immediately recognised my grandfather. And so that night became a spooky story my parents told at parties. It might have been my imagination, or a dream, but it's something I can't quite explain.'

'Stuff like that happens more than you'd think,' Anne said. 'All kids have moments when they can see beyond the usual spectrum. It's the brain chemistry sloshing around as they grow.'

'But you can still do it?'

'Yes.'

'Cool.'

'It's not as fun as you'd think.'

Sam could see the glow of the halogen lights creep around the bend in the tunnel. They were getting closer. They didn't teach you about this kind of thing at Hendon. His chest fluttered as the adrenalin kicked in. After the last couple of days, he'd tried to prepare himself mentally for anything that might lie around the corner. If a chorus of zombie clowns singing the works of Gilbert and Sullivan were waiting for him, he would expect it.

With a few more steps, Sam faced the otherworldly scene surrounding the train. Though the floodlights were still on, the area was deserted. Their pace quickened until they were alongside the first abandoned carriage. Sam relaxed slightly when no clowns, zombie or otherwise, appeared. He was unsettled, though, when they reached the gap in the cars. What had been dull rock in the tunnel wall now glistened with an eerie luminescence.

'Wormhole?' he asked Anne, his throat tight. Anne nodded. She reached out and the wall's surface rippled as if she had dropped a small pebble into a pond. Sam had seen nothing like it in his life. He now understood what it must've been like for great-great-great-grandad Graves when he'd seen the wonders he'd written about in his diary. Sam's world had suddenly grown larger. 'What do we do?' Sam asked. 'Just walk through?'

'Why are you asking me?'

'You're the expert consultant here.'

'Am I? The Met is going to get one hell of an invoice when this is all over, then.'

Sam held out his hand. Anne smiled and took it in hers.

'On three?' Sam asked.

'On three,' Anne repeated.

'One.'

'Two.'

'Three.'

Sam and Anne took one step forward, and their world grew a little larger still.

DAVE AND DEATH crashed through the door that led to the roof on which the top floor of UberSystems Tower lay. Just once, Dave thought, he would like to save the world from the ground floor, preferably whilst sat in a comfortable armchair.

'Where's the board room?' Death asked. Dave pointed upwards, to the highest window on the uppermost corner.

'There.'

'Of course it is. Why would anything be easy?'

'That's a good twenty metres' climb,' Dave said. 'What do you reckon?'

Death looked down the length of the tower to its base, resting near the chaos Oblivion was wreaking. 'I reckon we need to get a move on.'

They started their ascent, carefully picking their footholds and where to place their fingers. After only a few minutes, Death could feel the unfamiliar muscles in his limbs burning. He was glad he was in a body that hadn't skipped leg day at the gym.

'Why did you tell her you were Death?' Dave asked.

'Do we really need to discuss that now?'

'Laughing at your tragic love life is the only thing that's going to take my mind off the difficulty of this insane climb. So why did you tell her?'

'You told me once that you and Melanie try to be open with each other in your relationship, so I decided I should be honest with her.'

'Nothing good can come from taking relationship advice from me. You like her, then?'

'What's not to like?' asked Death. 'She's kind, smart, funny. We have similar interests.'

'If anything, you have interests that are polar opposites,' Dave replied. 'Her job is to keep people from going into the light and you actively encourage it.'

'Not anymore. It doesn't matter, anyway. She clearly thinks I'm mad.'

'Watching you brandish a flaming sword might change her perception of you.'

Death looked upwards, surprised to see how much ground they'd covered. Dave had been right, taking their mind off it had worked wonders. They were now only a few feet from the window closest to the boardroom's internal wall. 'With any luck, the sword should be in there.'

'I'll go in there,' Dave said. 'You carry on climbing to the top.'

Death groaned. 'Why me?'

'I can throw you the sword when I find it, and then you can walk down the side of the building. It's going to be a lot quicker than going back down to ground level.'

'Yeah, got to say I am missing the whole travelling-anywhere-instantaneously thing.'

With a few more strenuous pushes, they reached the shattered window. Dave dragged himself into the boardroom through the empty frame until he was resting safely against the wall.

Death kept moving upwards until he reached the top. He pulled himself up and collapsed onto the building, each ragged breath pulling pints of air into his scorched lungs. Some humans did this for entertainment, and they were all bonkers.

'You there?' Dave called from inside the building. Death staggered to his feet, unsteady on the slope. He looked down through a window and could barely make Dave out in the darkness below.

'Have you found it?'

'It's dark, but I've found something pointy.'

'Throw it up, then.'

'Okay, I'm doing it now. Make sure you catch it by the right end.'

The blade of a sword appeared out of the darkness before sinking back down. Death reeled backwards, almost losing his balance. Then there was a crash in the gloom as, Death guessed, Dave dived out of the way.

'Shit!' Dave called out.

'Are you alright?' Death shouted, concerned for his friend.

'Yeah, the bloody thing just embedded itself in the floor. Or the wall. I'm not sure how it works when a building's on its side. We haven't thought this through.'

'Let's give it one more try.'

'Fine. They're your fingers to lose.' There was the sound of a struggle as Dave pulled the sword loose. 'Okay, I've got it. After three. One, two, three.'

Death was ready this time. The pommel appeared first, and he reached out, wrapping his fingers around the sword's grip. He pulled the sword out and held it skyward in triumph. The blade ignited into an orange flame, the fire dancing off the slivers of glass at Death's feet. *I must look really cool,* he thought.

'Did you see that?' Death called down to Dave.

'Why? What did you do?'

I must look really cool and nobody bloody saw it, he thought.

'Hang on a minute,' Dave said. 'Wait for me.'

'No, Dave. This is something I must do alone. Get back down there and make sure everybody's safe.'

Silence for a moment, until Dave replied, 'Fine.'

Death turned away.

'Erm, just one thing?' said Dave.

'What is it?' Death called back.

'When this is all over, can I have a go with the sword?'

'Yes, as long as you're careful.'

As Dave thrust his fist in the air in exultation, Death walked away to meet his destiny.

'WHERE ON EARTH are we?' Sam asked.

'I don't think we're strictly on Earth anymore,' replied Anne.

The sky was as smooth and grey as slate. Gnarled trees, twisted by time, and snow highlighting the contours of the land, reminded Sam of the forests of the north. He sensed a darkness permeate this place. Ancient, terrible acts had been carried out here.

Whether or not they were on a different plane of reality, and the jury was out as far as Sam was concerned, they still had a job to do. 'Is there anything here that could eat us?' he asked.

Anne cast her eyes around. 'It all looks pretty dead to me.'

'Might as well go route one,' Sam said. He took a deep breath and shouted, 'Hello?' His voice bounced off the frozen trees and frigid rocks until it faded to nothing.

The reply that came back was weak and distant. One word: 'Help!'

Anne and Sam were as still as the landscape, trying to pinpoint where the voice had come from.

'Help!'

Anne pointed a way through the trees.

'There.'

EMMA AND KELVIN had freed the driver, named Rob. It was obvious his leg was broken, so Kelvin went into the nearest building to locate something that could be used as a splint and, if possible, some kind of makeshift stretcher.

Emma watched the news unfold on her phone. The channels had now got cameras on the top of the buildings surrounding UberSystems Plaza and the images cut from those to the camera on the drone hovering above the action.

'We still don't know who the individual is, or what they're doing,' said the news anchor over the images. 'It appears to be a young woman in her early twenties and—'

The camera's view jerked to the right, zoomed in, lost focus, then sharpened. The world watched Death striding with purpose down the side of a crashed skyscraper.

'Now we have another person. I'm not sure where he's come from, but he's walking down the side of the newly reappeared UberSystems Tower holding what appears to be a flaming sword. Can you confirm that, Sally?'

'Yes, Phil,' Sally replied. 'It seems to be a stabbing weapon of some variety. We can't verify what type, but it's definitely on fire.'

'The image is a tad fuzzy. Is he wearing a tee shirt suggesting we relax?'

'You're right, Phil. And while I appreciate the sentiment, I'm going to continue with the sense of panic I've been experiencing since this all started.'

'Your boyfriend's pretty hardcore,' Rob said. Emma couldn't hold back a smile.

'Yeah.'

DEATH COULDN'T HELP but think the city looked beautiful beneath its cage of lightning. A galaxy of lights seemed to move in time with the dancing electricity as shadows shifted around them. Much as he would've loved to stare at the scene forever, he had work to do. As he approached Oblivion, wormholes burned their way into reality like cigarettes through paper.

'Azrael! Oblivion! Whatever you call yourself!'

Oblivion looked up and then joined Death on the side of the tower. 'What are you doing here?'

Death shifted his grip on the sword, realising how ridiculous he must look to Oblivion. Here was a creature with the power to destroy worlds, and all Death had was an ancient weapon borrowed from a friend.

'I can't let you do this,' Death said. 'I can't let you kill all these people.'

'It's time we gave someone else a chance. Time we gave the world another chance, because it certainly won't survive this lot much longer.'

Death raised the flaming sword. Oblivion flicked a finger and Death flew backwards and landed further up the tower with bone-crunching force. He stayed flat on his back for a moment, looking up at a sky filling with rips and tears of nothingness, as if clawed by a giant mythological beast. The wormholes, gateways to a dark void, grew larger. There were probably only minutes left before they touched and formed a singularity that would wipe the earth clean of humanity. Death staggered to his feet. He tenderly felt the back of his head to find blood matting the hair. Such fragile bodies. He walked back to Oblivion. He was out of ideas, but at least he'd go down fighting.

With a wave of Oblivion's hand, Death found himself on his back again, this time with a greater impact. He was pretty sure his arm had broken that time. Pain, one of his oldest friends in this new life, travelled from his shoulder to his useless fingers.

'Why are you doing this? I'll let you live. I'll let the female live. What was her name? Emma?' said Oblivion, genuinely confused. 'You said yourself they're an angry, useless, feckless, fickle, baffling species.'

Death hesitated for a moment. Oblivion's offer would be the easier option. The world would belong to him and Emma. They would have a lifetime to get to know each other. But that wasn't the man he was.

The game was over. No human could defeat Oblivion. If Death had been in his previous form, a form that had defeated even Beelzebub himself, they might have a chance. Then he remembered something; an idea lurching out of the fog of a drunken evening. It may or may not work, but what did it matter now?

Using the sword as a crutch, Death climbed to his tired feet. He stumbled to the edge of the building. What had Dave called it? A leap of faith? Death turned to the drone hovering nearby. With his good hand, he gave a thumbs up.

Yes, it was a beautiful city. It was a beautiful world. It would have been beautiful to be a part of it.

He jumped.

'HOW MUCH LONGER have we got left?' Sam asked. Anne checked her watch.

'About ten minutes.'

They continued in the voice's direction. A voice that had gone ominously silent. New wormholes, windows hanging in the air, appeared the deeper they walked into the dead forest.

Sam waved at the voids carved into the universe. 'Where do you think these go to?'

'No idea. Could be anywhere,' replied Anne, her eyes focused forward, concentrating on where she was heading. 'Don't touch anything.'

The Other Place that they were in had once been lush and vibrant. The land, sea and sky had all been thick with life until nature had called it a day and hit the brakes. But not everything had died. While the surface was frozen and barren, beneath the permafrost something stirred from its slumber. It had been so long since it had smelt the sweet aroma of fresh meat. The creature stretched powerful limbs and dragged itself from its nest towards the light of the surface.

'Are we there yet?'

Anne took a deep breath. 'Yes, Sam. Just over this next hill. I'm sure of it.'

'You said that three hills ago.'

Anne was turning around to start an argument that had been brewing since two hills back when a twig snapped. She froze, and in that stillness heard the raking of branches behind them. The crunch and tear of foliage carried in the dead air as something of substantial weight and strength stalked them.

Then Anne saw it, something that looked like a giant lizard had mated with a Venus Flytrap. Innumerable rows of teeth sliced and slashed the frigid air as the monster charged. Before Anne's brain could comprehend what was happening, her legs made an executive decision and were already taking her over the hill.

Sam's laboured breath told her he was close and, further back, the regulated beat of four muscular legs meant that the monster wasn't far behind either. Fear propelled Anne forward. For a fraction of a second, she thought that all she needed to do to get out of this situation was be faster than Sam. Then, she felt something long jab into her chest.

Gary's Peperami. Anne pulled it from her jacket's inside pocket and stripped away the foil wrapping, revealing the tough brown stick inside. Not looking back, she threw it over her shoulder and there was a scrape of leaves as the monster skidded to a halt. That should give them a bit of time.

It was then that Anne saw a flash among the darkened hues of the Other Place: the train carriage.

'There!' Anne shouted to Sam, changing direction down a shallow incline. They covered the ground in a few seconds and were soon at one of the red sliding doors that had been jimmied open. The passengers had deserted the carriage and the surrounding area. The perfectly round mouth of a wormhole hovered in front of the carriage.

'Do you reckon they went through there?' Sam wheezed, waving at the wormhole. 'Wherever they've gone, they were in a state of mind to take all their possessions with them.'

A deep-throated growl reminded Anne they weren't alone. She turned to face the flytrap lizard. Its many mouths drooled in anticipation of its next meal. All Anne had done was whet its appetite.

'I can't run anymore,' Sam said. 'I reckon we take our chances with the wormhole.'

'We don't know where we'll end up,' replied Anne.

'Yeah, but I know where we'll end up in the next few seconds if we don't do *something*.' Sam nodded towards the creature prowling towards them. Anne had to admit that he was right. Better to take their chances with the vagaries of the space-time continuum than hang around here.

'Won't it just follow us?'

'Hang on. I've got a spare,' Sam said, pulling a Peperami from his jacket.

'We're going to have to buy Gary a supply of those to say thank you,' said Anne as Sam tore at the foil wrapper, peeling it away from the meat. The monster hungrily watched as Sam waved it from side to side.

'Godspeed, you weird, weird snack.' Sam threw the salami high and far. It span end-over-end, the flytrap lizard chasing after it like an eager puppy until it landed in a patch of snow.

'Alright,' Anne said. 'Let's go.'

Anne and Sam turned on their heels and ran for the wormhole. They leapt in and slipped away from the Other Place.

When the flytrap lizard had devoured the Peperami, it looked up to find Anne and Sam gone. With a growl of frustration, it turned around and headed back to its nest to dream of dried meat snack foods.

CARROLL HAD WATCHED Sam and Anne disappear into the tunnel on a control room monitor, then turned his attention to the laptop and installed the software patch. Once he'd finished that, it was a matter of disabling all the safety protocols that would spring into action as soon as he ran the code.

Rose insisted on helping, so Carroll had her prepare the Thingummy in the other room. He experienced a little thrill of excitement when he asked her to reverse the polarity of the power couplings, like he was in an episode of Star Trek.

'When you're done with that, I want you out of here,' Caroll told her through the intercom. 'I've got no idea what'll happen when this thing gets going.'

'Will do. I'm pretty much done here.' Rose smiled and gave a thumbs up through the glass. That smile vanished, though, when she saw something over Carroll's shoulder.

'Stop what you're doing,' a familiar voice said from behind Carroll, followed by the metallic click of a gun being cocked. Carroll removed his hands from the laptop's keyboard.

'Turn around.' Carroll slowly spun his chair around and stared down the barrel of a pistol. Behind that stood Captain Mills. When Carroll remembered what he had done this morning, he thought Mills looked understandably cross.

'What are you doing here, Mills?'

'Stopping you doing whatever it is you're getting up to.' Mills nodded to a monitor showing the carnage outside.

'If you don't let me get on with this, then *everything everyone* is getting up to will stop.'

'I've got my orders to bring you in.'

'But the people giving the orders aren't aware of the full situation. There's a very good chance that the entire world is going to end, but we can sort this out. I just need to press the return key on this computer.' Carroll started to turn back to the desk, but Mills raised the gun so it was aimed directly between Carroll's eyes. Carroll stopped his spin and returned to facing Mills. 'Or we can talk some more. Look, why don't you get the minister on the telephone and I can walk her through everything?'

'Where are your accomplices?' Mills asked, ignoring everything Carroll had said. Carroll groaned impatiently.

'We don't have time for this. Didn't you join the army to protect this country? Here's your chance.'

188

'Stand up.' Carroll sat forward, looked Mills in the eyes.

'This is your last chance to do the right thing.'

'No, this is *your* last chance,' Mills said, aggression creeping in at the edges of the words. Carroll sat back in his chair.

'OK, Dave. You can hit him.'

Mills turned and the side of his head met the computer keyboard as Dave swung it with all his strength. In an explosion of plastic keys and springs, Mills spun around, the gun falling from his hand and skittering across the floor.

Carroll was out of his seat before Mills could work out what had happened. He picked up the gun and aimed it inexpertly at Mills's bloody face. Dave joined him at his side.

'I hope you don't mind me letting myself in, but the door was open. So, this is a secret underground government research lab?'

'Yep.'

'Nice.'

'How's it looking out there?'

'Two angels of death are fighting on the side of a skyscraper that just crash-landed from another dimension. Your average Wednesday evening in East London.'

Mills checked his nose and jaw for damage, his breath shallow and ragged. 'I think I've swallowed a crown. Do you know how much that'll cost to replace? You are so dead when this is over.'

'Mate, if you knew the kind of week I'd had, you'd realise how little that threat bothers me,' replied Dave in a low growl. Maybe there was still some wolf left in him.

Carroll waved the gun at a chair further along the bank of desks. 'Whatever. Sit down there.' Mills, sulking, did as he was told. Carroll returned to his laptop, careful not to take his eyes off Mills. 'Have you heard from Anne or DCI Graves?'

'No, where are they?' Dave replied.

'They went into the tunnel.'

'How long can we wait before we start the shutdown?'

'Not for much longer,' replied Carroll as his mobile phone rang. He answered it. 'Hello?' Carroll looked at Dave, relief written all over his face. 'It's DCI Graves.' He returned his attention to the phone call.

'I'm sorry, you're *where*?'

EYES OPEN. STAYING open. No more broken limbs or leaking bodily fluids. No weak flesh enveloped in delicate skin. Cloaked in cloth as black as midnight, he was once again Death in both name and form.

He looked at the broken body lying next to him. It stared back blankly. Steve Newman was dead, returned to being an unidentified corpse; a spent vessel. He thanked it silently for all it had allowed him to do.

The sky was still full of holes and light. It was not over yet. Death picked up the sword by his feet. What was that phrase Dave often used that annoyed Anne so much? Oh yeah.

Let's fuck shit up.

FIVE MINUTES EARLIER, Sam and Anne had tumbled behind the curtains between worlds until they were spat out onto a cold, hard floor.

'Where are we?' asked Sam.

'I don't know. I haven't opened my eyes yet,' Anne replied.

'Neither have I. Can you hear music?'

'It's not just me, then?' said Anne, relieved. 'Is it Sacha Distel?'

'I'm opening my eyes,' Sam said. 'OK, it's pitch black. I don't know if that's good or bad.'

A door opened and light spilled over mops, dustpans and ant-bacterial sprays.

'Qu'est ce que tu fais ici?' a shadow in the doorway asked. Sam looked over at the dimly-lit shape he assumed was Anne.

'In a world of infinite possibilities, we've ended up in a Frenchman's broom cupboard?'

The shadow fumbled for a switch on the wall and they were bathed in a sterile light from an unshaded bulb, surrounded by shelves heavy with cleaning products. A man in a white shirt, bow tie and polite smile stood over Anne and Sam, who were sprawled on the floor between some buckets.

'You are English, yes?'

Anne nodded. 'Yes. Where are we?'

'The rest of your party has just arrived. Would you care to join them?' The Frenchman helped Sam and Anne to their feet, dusting them down. He led them out of the cupboard and down a narrow hallway filled with cans of vegetable oil. To their left was a bustling kitchen, and the door at the end of the hall opened up into a small bistro where waiters glided between the white-clothed tables.

'It is lovely weather, so we've sat you outside,' the waiter said as he led them out onto the pavement and the cool night. The staff had hurriedly shoved several tables together and around them sat fourteen grubby and tired diners, all studying menus. Sam had to admire the French service. Over a dozen people had dropped into their restaurant from another dimension, and they didn't even blink.

'Is that the Eiffel Tower?' Anne asked, grabbing Sam's shoulder. The iron structure rose from behind the white-washed Parisian appartements across the street. It really was a rue with a view. Sam turned to the middle-aged woman sat nearest to him at the end of the table.

'Excuse me, you haven't just fallen out of a wormhole after a train carriage you'd been travelling on ended up in a fantastical land, have you?'

'Are you from Transport for London?' the woman replied, looking up from her menu. 'Because a few of us would like to make complaints.'

'No, I'm DCI Graves from the Met. Could I have your name?'

'Sandra Faulkner.' Sam recognised the name from a list he'd seen. He'd done his job and found the passengers. 'Excuse us, but we've only had Jeff's multipack of Iced Gems to keep us going for the past two days.'

Sam cleared his throat. He should probably say something reassuring. 'Ladies and gentlemen, my name's DCI Graves. Remain calm. We'll be getting you back home as soon as we can.'

The occupants of the table looked at each other. 'Not before I have a glass of Pinot and some calamari,' somebody shouted.

Sam didn't know what to do next. Going back to London the way they came wasn't a possibility. Going via the Channel would take too long. Whatever Dave, Kelvin and Carroll were going to do, they were on their own. He'd got his job done, at least. He could take comfort in that.

'What do we do now?' he asked Anne.

Sam stepped out of the way as two waiters placed another table next to Sandra. The waiters placed two chairs on either side and offered them to him and Anne.

'Monsieur? Madame?'

Anne looked at Sam, then shrugged and sat down, accepting a menu from the waiter.

'I say we have that drink. A proper one, this time,' she said with a smile.

Sam laughed. Either he'd gone mad, or everybody else had. If there was a chance the world was going to end, he might as well go out eating a decent steak.

'I just need to make a quick phone call.'

CARROLL PUT THE phone down. 'They're in Paris,' he said to Dave.

'Lovely time of the year for it. Have they found the passengers?'

'They have.'

'Nothing stopping us from wrapping things up our end, then?' Rose said as she walked into the control room.

'I guess there isn't,' Carroll replied. His finger hovered over the return key on the laptop's keyboard. He looked from Rose to Dave to Mills. 'Ready?'

Rose and Dave nodded. Mills just shrugged. Carroll pressed the key.

A low hum filled the room as the Thingummy sprang into life. Rose and Carroll watched the computer as readouts started scrolling up the screen. The noise rose in pitch as the Thingummy's work rate increased.

'We're close to redlining,' Rose said.

'It's okay,' Carroll replied. 'I expected that.'

'But isn't there a chance of a runaway causal nexus leading to a temporal collapse?'

'What does that mean? It doesn't sound good,' said Dave.

'There's a chance that time itself might stop and then be destroyed,' Carroll explained. 'But I'm pretty sure that won't happen.'

'Please don't make time explode.'

'Actually, it would be more of an implosion,' Rose said.

'Well, that makes all the difference.'

The Thingummy juddered, and the hum turned into a scream that hovered on the threshold of the range of human hearing. The device glowed with white heat, and thin wisps of smoke leaked from the joints of the power couplings.

'I'll admit, I wasn't expecting that,' Carroll said. 'Hold this.' He passed the gun to Dave, who pointed it at Mills. Carroll headed to the Thingummy's room, striding with purpose.

'If you kill us all, I'm going to be so cross with you,' Mills called after him.

'I've got it under control,' Carroll said as he walked through the heavy door between the two rooms, closing it behind him. He circled the Thingummy, inspecting each section. He stopped and placed a finger on his pursed lips, deep in thought. Reaching a conclusion, he nodded and walked out the door on the other side of the room.

'Is the bloody coward running away?' Mills asked. A few seconds passed and Carroll returned with a large wrench. He delicately adjusted one nut on the Thingummy, then raised the wrench above his head and brought it down full force on one of the power leads. The noise immediately dropped several octaves and returned to a steady, low hum.

Rose looked at the data on the computer screen. 'That's done it,' she said. Carroll stepped back into the room.

'Everything good now?'

'Readings are back within acceptable parameters,' Rose said.

'That was your brilliant idea?' Mills said. 'Hit it with a bloody great spanner?'

'The technical term is percussive maintenance,' Carroll corrected him. 'Let's get this finished, shall we?'

'YOU ARE PERSISTENT, I'll give you that,' Oblivion said when Death had joined her on UberSystems Tower.

'I learnt it from them.' Death waved a hand at the world.

'This is your true form, then?' Death nodded. 'It suits you.' Oblivion looked to the sky. 'You're too late, though. Soon it'll be me and you alone.'

Death raised the sword. He would not fall again.

'The thing is, I have many forms,' Oblivion said with a grin, no longer resembling a young woman but a hideous creature Death believed would be happy destroying everything. Towering over Death, Oblivion smiled, revealing a mouth lined with knife-like teeth. Her innumerable clawed hands reached for his cloak. Though Death tried to retreat, Oblivion got some purchase and tugged at the cape, flinging Death clear of UberSystems Tower. Before he hit the ground, Death transported himself back to the spot Oblivion had thrown him from. He knew Oblivion was toying with him; keeping him busy until the plan was complete.

Death charged, flaming sword held aloft to deal a terrible blow, but Oblivion forced him back once more. He regrouped his scattered thoughts, marshalling one or two which were making a break for freedom. There had to be a way in through Oblivion's attacks. As Death circled Oblivion, probing for weaknesses, a shrill vibrato sound cut through the air. It took Death a moment to realise it was the old mobile phone that he'd taken with him that morning. He found it in the folds of his cloak and answered it.

'Hello?'

'Hiya. It's Dave,' the voice said on the other end.

'Oh, hello. What do you want? I'm in the middle of something.'

'Yeah, yeah, we can see. Big scary monster vibes.' Oblivion leaned in, 'Are we doing this, or…'

Death put his hand over the mouthpiece. 'Do you mind? I'm in the middle of a phone call.' He turned his attention back to the phone. 'Carry on, Dave.'

'I was just phoning to say Dr Carroll's invoked the shutdown protocol so you've got about thirty seconds to keep Oblivion distracted.'

'Invoked the shutdown protocol?'

'He ran a software update. I just wanted to sound cool. Good luck.' Dave hung up.

If the wormholes closed, Death was sure Oblivion would just take humanity one by one. Sure, it would take longer, but that wasn't a concern when time had no meaning. They'd chase each other across the world, jumping from place to place until one of them was the victor. How many lives would suffer?

That gave Death an idea. With a warrior's cry, he charged at Oblivion one last time, bringing the sword down and then thrusting it forward. As Oblivion swung one of her mighty paws, Death disappeared, jumping a few inches forward so he was out of range of the heavy blow. Oblivion overreached and fell forward onto Death's sword, letting forth an inhuman scream as it punctured the skin. Death leaned forward so Oblivion could hear every word.

'They might be an angry, useless, feckless, fickle, baffling species, but they're *my* angry, useless, feckless, fickle, baffling species.'

Death pushed a stunned Oblivion away. Disorientated, the monster staggered backwards until she stepped into thin air. Tumbling down, her howls shredded the air from London to Tokyo and back again, until she fell into one of the many wormholes circling the plaza.

A second later, the universe glitched and stuttered. The wormholes quietly imploded, winking out of existence, thousands of tears in the fabric of reality repairing themselves instantly.

Death watched the lightning grow weaker until it petered out into nothing. The night was still and dark as if Death, the tower and the body beneath were the only things that existed.

DEATH STOOD ALONE in the multitude, ignored by those that passed by. Humans often cannot see what they don't want to. It's in their nature. Already it was just like old times for him, like slipping into some familiar clothes.

The crowd parted and there was Emma. She and Kelvin had got Rob treatment, and now she was running triage for the medical services set up away from UberSystems Plaza. Death watched her comfort the wounded and the frightened for hours until they forced her to take a break. She grabbed a coffee and found a bench in a small, quiet park.

Death stepped out from the shadows and instantly regretted his choice of entrance. Emma looked up from her drink and turned deathly white.

'Don't be afraid,' Death said.

'That's easy for you to say,' Emma replied. 'You're not staring at your worst nightmare.'

'Charming.'

'This is a strong look. Those clothes new?' Emma said, the colour returning to her cheeks. Death admired her bravery.

'How are you?' asked Death.

'Well, I watched a man I liked called Steve Newman fall to his death a little while ago. How do you think I am? Who was he?'

'He was Adam Thorpe.' Death remembered it all now. 'He was kind enough to help me when I was at my lowest. Let them know his name.'

'And who are you?'

'I am Death. The whisper on the lips of the damned. The dark companion who walks in the shadows of humanity's souls.'

Emma nodded. She understood. Death was always impressed by a human's ability to adapt to a new situation, no matter how bizarre they thought it was. 'Good to meet you. If you're here, where is *she* now?'

'Azrael? The nothingness she brought forth into this world consumed her.'

Emma sat back on the bench. 'Your speech is a lot more grandiose when you're like this.'

'I have an image to maintain.'

'Why are you here?'

'To say thank you and goodbye.'

'Thank you for what?'

'For being you. Perhaps I had taken humanity for granted, forgotten why I was here, but you have shown me what they can be like. I don't think we can continue this, though. It's not you, it's me.'

Emma laughed. 'It's probably for the best. It would just be awkward if I was to ever introduce you to my parents.'

'I have to go.'

'Will we meet again?'

'Yes. Once more.'

'You're really sucking the joy out of being dumped by the personification of death, you know that?'

'I'm sorry, it's my first time.'

'It's okay. Can I ask one favour?'

'Anything. It's the least I can do.'
'Can I see what's under your hood?'

THE THINGUMMY SHUT off; the hum winding down and its hot metal plating creaking as it cooled.

Carroll checked the numbers on the computer screen. 'Looks like the wormholes and interdimensional tears have been sealed. We did it.'

'Well done, doc,' Dave said, patting him on the back.

'Perhaps you should make yourself scarce. The authorities will be down here soon and you hit a senior officer in the army around the head with a computer keyboard.'

'He's right,' Mills said. 'I am going to have to pound on you a little.'

'What are you going to do?' Dave asked Carroll, ignoring the captain.

'Somebody's going to have to do some explaining. I think it's best that I stay around.'

'Good luck.' Dave offered his hand and Carroll shook it.

BACK ON THE surface, Dave called home to speak to Melanie and Gary, who was excitable as a child on Christmas morning.

'Listen to this,' Gary said. ' "Serious questions are being asked of defence secretary Lorraine Arden after leaked classified documents revealed she had allowed government experiments blamed for the scenes of destruction witnessed in the capital earlier today." That's on the BBC website. That was us. We did that.'

'Well done. I'm very proud of you, but isn't the BBC fake news?' Dave asked.

'It's only fake news if I don't agree with it,' Gary said. Dave shook his head in exasperation.

'Can you put Melanie on, please?'

'Hi, babe,' Melanie said when Gary had passed the phone over. 'Are you okay?'

'I'm fine. Everyone's safe here now. How are you?'

'It's all good here. Are you coming home soon?'

'I might stay here for a bit. It looks like they need help. The place looks like Gary's bedroom.'

'I heard that,' Gary shouted down the phone.

'Any sign of Steve?' Melanie asked.

'Not yet. I'll see what I can find out and I'll let you know when I'm on my way back.'

'Okay. I love you.' Dave smiled.

'I love you, too.'

DAVE FOUND DEATH in a playground. To anyone else, it looked like the swing was moving in a breeze, but the Grim Reaper swayed back-and-forth, his gaze fixed on the ground in front of him.

'Hello. Where have you been?' Dave asked as he sat on the swing next to Death. Death looked up, brought out of his haze.

'Oh, hello Dave. I had some things to sort out. Been up to anything nice since I left you?'

'Helping clean things up. We made a bit of a mess of the city.'

'And there's you complaining when Anne asks you to tidy your desk. Have you heard from her?'

'She's in Paris.'

'Paris?'

'Wormholes, apparently.'

'Must've been a bloody big worm.'

'She's taking a couple of days leave.'

'Good for her. Paris is a wonderful city. It certainly has fewer buildings falling out of the sky than London. What are they saying about me on the news?'

'That you're just some mysterious hooded figure.'

'That'll do, I suppose.'

'Thanks for saving the human race and all that.'

'No problem.'

'Have you spoken to Emma?'

'Yes.'

'How'd it go?'

Death sighed. 'It was difficult. Have you ever had to do that?'

'I was usually on the receiving end,' replied Dave, 'but it's not great from either side. I'll tell you what we'll do. We'll get some beers in, maybe a pizza, and watch Die Hard.'

'That sounds great, but I've got a lot of catching up to do,' Death said. Dave smiled.

'You're back on the team, then?'

'Yes.'

'Glad to have you back.'

'Glad not to have to use a toilet again.'

'And do I get my job back?'

'As far as I am concerned, you never left.'

'Brilliant. Can I have a go with the sword now?'

'I lost it again.'

'Aw, bloody hell. Will you give me a lift home, then?'

'Sure, but I need to swing by the office to pick something up first.'

'IT'S IN MY office,' Death said when they arrived at One Crow Road. 'Won't be a minute.'

When Death had disappeared behind his office door, Dave noticed a shoebox on the edge of Anne's desk. "WARS STUFF. KEEP OUT." was scrawled on the lid. Curious, he removed the lid and fished through the contents, which were mostly bullets and military medals, until he came to something altogether more delicate. Dave teased a thin, silver chain free from the handle of a small switchblade knife around which it was caught. A charm was attached; a small red, green and silver Christmas bauble that spun as he held it up to the light.

There was something captivating about the cheap trinket. Why would War have something so dainty and fragile amongst his possessions? From what Dave had been told of him, he was a big bearded immortal being who liked to hit people over the head with blunt instruments.

Take it.

A voice in his head, unbidden. The pendant's owner was decades gone. It belonged to no-one. Why shouldn't he? Unable to help himself, he took the bauble between his thumb and forefinger. For a fraction of a second he had an urge to squeeze hard until it shattered into a thousand sharp shards. The thought scared him for reasons he didn't comprehend.

Take it.

He slipped the necklace over his head, tucked it under his tee shirt, and let the bauble settle on his chest. His heartbeat quickened and his head swam and it appeared the universe had shifted. The feeling soon passed as Death walked into the room carrying a scythe with a blade so sharp it could cut time.

'What do you think?' he asked. 'I knew I had a spare somewhere.'

Dave smiled. 'You look great.'

'Right, let's get you home.'

Dave was about to replace the lid on the box when something caught his eye.

'Uh, Death?'

'Yes?'

'Do you know how to disarm a hand grenade?'

Printed in Great Britain
by Amazon